ALMOST BLUE

ALMOST BLUE

CARLO LUCARELLI

TRANSLATED BY OONAGH STRANSKY

CITY LIGHTS BOOKS
SAN FRANCISCO

First City Lights edition Copyright (c) 2001 by City Lights Books
Copyright (c) 1997 by Giulio Einaudi eidtore s.p.a., Torino, Italy
Translation (c) 2001 by Oonagh Stransky

Cover design: Amy Trachtenberg / Robin Raschke
Book design: Nancy J. Peters
Typography: Harvest Graphics

This publication was assisted by the Italian Ministry of Foreign
Affairs through the Istituto Italiano di Cultura, San Francisco
(Director: Amelia Antonucci).

Library of Congress Cataloging-in-Publication Data

Lucarelli, Carlo, 1960-
      [Almost blue. English]
      Almost blue / Carlo Lucarelli ; translated from the Italian
by Oonagh Stransky.
          p.   cm.
      ISBN 0-87286-389-1
      I. Stransky, Oonagh.
   PQ4872.U255 A8213 2001
   853'.914—dc21   2001042127

CITY LIGHTS BOOKS are edited by Lawrence Ferlinghetti
and Nancy J. Peters and published at the City Lights Bookstore,
261 Columbus Avenue, San Francisco CA 94133.
www.citylights.com

The first Carabiniere to enter the room slipped on the blood and fell to his knees. The second one stopped short in the doorway as if at the edge of a pit, his arms extended to keep his balance.

"Madonna Santa!" he exclaimed, covering his face with his hands. He turned and ran back down the hall, down the stairs, and out the front door to the parking lot where he'd left the black-and-white Fiat Punto patrol car. He leaned heavily on the hood, doubled over with nausea.

Alone on his knees in the middle of the room, his leather gloves stuck to the slippery floor, Brigadiere Carrone of the Carabinieri Corps glanced around. He retched drily, with a belching sound. When he tried to stand up, his heels slipped out from underneath him and he sat back down hard and then, with a viscous smack, fell onto his side. He tried to prop himself up but his hand slipped, leaving a lighter streak on the reddened tiles. He wound up on his back, unable to move, as if trapped in a nightmare.

He shut his eyes and floundered wildly, arms and legs flailing in the air like a cockroach stranded on its back. Then, splattering blood everywhere, he opened his mouth and began to scream.

Part One

ALMOST BLUE

*Almost blue, almost doing things
we used to do.*
                    —Elvis Costello, "Almost Blue"

The sound of a record dropping onto a turntable is like a short sigh, with a touch of dust mixed in. The sound of the automated arm rising up from its rest is like a repressed hiccup or a tongue clucking drily—a plastic tongue. The needle, as it glides across the grooves, sibilates softly and crackles once or twice. Then comes the piano, a dripping faucet. Then, the bass, buzzing like an enormous fly at a window. Finally, the velvety voice of Chet Baker singing "Almost Blue.".

If you listen carefully, you can almost hear him taking a breath and opening his mouth to sing the first *A* in *Almost*. It sounds so tight it seems more like a long *O*. *Al–most–blue* . . . with two pauses. He takes two breaths. You just know—you can tell—that his eyes are closed.

That's why I like "Almost Blue"; you have to sing it with your eyes closed.

My eyes are closed even when I'm not singing. I'm blind. I've been blind since I was born. I've never seen colors or light or movement of any kind.

I listen.

I scan the silence around me the way an electronic scanner sweeps the airwaves for sounds and voices, tuning automatically into any and all frequencies. I know how to use both my scanners perfectly, the internal one that I've had in my head for the past twenty-five years, ever since I was born, and the electric one in my room next to my stereo. If I had any friends, I know they'd call me Scanner. I'd like that.

But I don't have any friends. It's my own fault. I just don't understand them. They talk about things that have nothing to do with me, they use words like lucid, opaque, luminous, invisible. Like in the bedtime story that my parents used to tell me when I was little to help me fall asleep — there was a beautiful princess whose skin was so clear it seemed transparent. I spent many sleepless nights wondering about that word before I understood that transparent means you can see into it.

For me, it means that you can poke your fingers through it.

Colors, too, have different meanings for me. Colors have a voice, colors make sounds, just like other things, so that I can distinguish between them. Identify them. Understand them. Azure, for example, with that *z* in the middle, is the color of *z*abaglione, *z*ebras, and *z*innias. *V*ases, *v*iolins, and *v*ixen are all *v*iolet; a loud *yell* is always *yell*ow. I can't imagine *b*lack but I know it is the color of *b*arrenness, of *b*leakness, the black hole of emptiness.

But it's not just a question of alliteration. Some colors signify the very idea that they contain. For the *sound* of the idea inside them. Green, with that harsh *r* sound that scratches and flares its way out of the middle of the word, is the color of something that scathes and burns, like the sun. But blue, on the other hand, is the color of beauty. For example, for me, a pretty girl might have blonde hair, but a truly beautiful girl would be *b*arefoot, *b*rave, and have *blue* hair.

Some colors even have shapes. Something large and round is definitely red. But shapes aren't as interesting; I don't understand them. To understand them, you have to touch them, and I don't like touching things or people. Besides, you can only touch things that are nearby. By listening and imagining I can travel further. I like sounds better.

That's why I use my scanner. Every night I go up to my room in the attic and put on Chet Baker. I always put on the same record because I like the sound of his trumpet, all those deep, precise *p* sounds. I like the way he sings slowly, the way his voice seems to come from a place somewhere behind his throat. You can tell it's hard for him to find his voice and that to find it he has to close his eyes and concentrate really hard. "Almost Blue" is my favorite song. I always play it first, even though it's the last track on the record. I wait all day for that moment at night when the trumpet, the bass, the piano, and his voice come together and fill the emptiness inside my head.

Then I turn on the scanner and listen to the city.

I've never seen Bologna, but I know it well, even if it's probably my own imaginary Bologna. It's a big city: almost three hours.

I know that, because once I tuned to the CB radio of a truck and followed it for the whole time it was within the range of my scanner. The truck driver never stopped talking on it, from the moment he first appeared on the scanner until he disappeared. He talked his way across the city.

—"Breaker 1-9, this is Rambo—come in. Breaker 1-9, this is Rambo—anyone out there? . . . I'm at the Rimini–South exit, watch out, Customs agents are pulling people over . . .

—"This is Rambo, come in Diablo . . . listen, I know where you can get an amazing blow job. Exit at Casa-lecchio di Reno, take the service road, go to the gas station on the corner. Ask for Luana."

—"This is Rambo. Who is this, Maradona? What do you mean, El Diablo is pissed off? Didn't he know Luana was a transvestite? You can tell him I'm stopping at Parma 2 for the night, I'll meet him there . . . and tell him to go fu—. . ."

And then, suddenly, the voices stop. My city has a well-defined perimeter; it's bordered by silence. On the other side of the border there's an abyss that swallows up all sounds, blacker than black. Emptiness.

Sometimes I tune in to the police channel and listen to the squad cars calling headquarters. I feel like I'm suspended above the city, that I have many ears and that I can hear all the voices at once.

—"Car 4 to Base: we have a serious accident on the Via Emilia . . . we need an ambulance right away . . . code 9."

—"Car 2 to Base . . . we're at the Banca Cooperativa, the alarm is ringing but everything looks quiet . . ."

—"Run a check on these plates: A for Ancona; D, Domodossola . . ."

—"OK, the guy is clean, but the girl's a minor and has no ID, what's the procedure?"

—"Message received. We're on our way."

—"It looks like an overdose. Shit, this guy's going to die in the car."

—"Siena–Monza 5–1 . . . Siena-Monza 5-1 . . ."

—"Come in Siena-Monza . . ."

—"We're on Via Filopanti, at the corner of Via Galliera, we've picked up *una negra* with no ID. . . ."

The cop's voice is strong, but all nose, as if he has a cold. In the background I can hear the green drone of passing cars and the blue buzz of *motorini*. Farther away, underneath it all, so deep that it almost gets confused with Chet Baker's trumpet, I can discern sharp voices that prick the surface ever so slightly.

—"No, I no come with you. You no right, I no come . . ."

—"Hey, get back here, where the fuck do you think you're going? You want me to hit you again?" a strong red voice says.

When I've had enough and feel like listening to a story, I tune in to cell phone conversations.

—"Hey, what's that guy with the headphones doing?"

I hear music. Distant music. Throbbing, synthesized drums, filtered by something thick, like a wall. In the foreground, I hear the green hum of a GSM phone. Speaking into it is a second voice, mellifluous and liquid, that rolls its *L*s and *R*s.

—"Shit, I think I'm stuck . . . hello? Hey, listen, Lalla—where the hell is the rave? Nobody here knows anything about it . . ."

—"What the hell is that guy with the headphones doing?"

This voice is different, less liquid, hazier, smoky, like thick fog. It's situated somewhere between the pulsing, distant music and the voice talking into the GSM.

—"Hey, Tasso . . . what do you think that guy with the headphones is doing?"

—"Damn it, Misero . . . how the hell do I know? He's probably a bouncer . . ."

—"It looks like he's recording something . . ."

—"So, he's probably a soundman . . . Hey, Lalla? Are you still there? Shit, Misero. He hung up! Now who's going to tell us where the rave is?"

—"Let's ask the soundman."

—"Do that, why don't you? Go ahead, go ask the soundman. Hello, Lalla, you still there?"

—"Hey, Tasso, he's not a soundman, he's a total freak,

he says he's got some really good grass. I wonder what the hell he's doing with those headphones . . ."

When the story gets boring or when I don't understand it any more, I press a little button and skim across the waves until I find something more interesting. Sometimes I do it all night; when you can't see sunlight it doesn't matter if you sleep during the day or night. I just keep scanning the darkness, sometimes even crossing statical paths with other scanners. Listening to the voice of the city.

When I get sleepy I turn it off.

Silence. The soft rustling sound of silence.

And Chet Baker, singing "Almost Blue."

"What the hell is that guy with the headphones doing?"

I'm cold and naked.

I look at my reflection in the red puddle that has formed under the bed. The animal is still slithering under my skin, distorting my face. I pick up part of the African mask that fell off the wall and cover my face with it so I don't have to see it anymore.

But I can still hear them.

The bells from hell. They ring constantly, day and night, they toll through my head and bones as if my brain itself was a living bell, cracking and pealing with every knell. Sometimes the bells come from far away, near the nape of my neck. When it's like that I only hear their echo, a metallic clanging expands inside me, a thin ring of sound. Then they start ringing higher up again, near the center of my head. They toll through my nose and teeth and reverberate off my forehead, tearing at the joints in my bones, splitting open my cranium. I hear death bells. Day and night. Ringing for the dead and ringing for me.

I put on the headphones of my Walkman to muffle the sound, but it's not enough. I look down: the wire hangs down my chest, the jack dangles inertly between my legs. I turn on the stereo, bass and treble on max, the volume all the way up, the LED completely red, not even flashing. I reach for the jack and shove it into the socket—a wall goes up inside my head, hard and compact, from ear to ear behind my eyes. The drums, the snare, and the plates rattle through my head like a snake's tongue. The guitar is a bombardment of electrifying rain, the bass guitar like wild thunder that gets closer and closer, the singer's voice breaks like lightning across the sky in a deadening scream. There's a wall in my head—a *Wall*. The bells ring against it, deadened. Each peal gets a little farther away. I go over to the bunkbed, the headphone wire as taut as a leash. I pull my knees into my chest. The goosebumps on my cold, smooth legs rub up against my nipples.

I'm cold and naked. The clothes I was wearing I tore to shreds. The ones on the floor got so drenched that now they're as hard as cardboard. I curl up on the edge of the bed and rest my head on a corner of the pillow where the drops falling from the mattress above won't drip on me. The rest of the bed is soaked.

I'm cold and naked and curled up in a ball. If I stuck a syringe in my heart, I'm sure the blood that would come pumping out would be as black as India ink. I can imagine it bubbling up under the piston, thick and dense, rippling it with opaque bubbles and painting the sides of the cylinder. If I stuck a syringe in my heart I'm sure the pressure I feel inside me would make it explode in a black gush of crude oil. There's something pushing against my ribcage and at my throat. It slithers out of my heart and under my skin, toward my throat. Maybe if I open my mouth the animal will slide out over my tongue and between my teeth.

I sit up and squeeze the Sony headphones closer to my head. The bells have returned and are even louder now. I rock back and forth, elbows on my knees, hands on the headphones. I'm cold and naked. Really cold. I slide down to the floor and crawl across the room on all fours, carefully, so I don't cut myself on the broken glass from the bottle or the alarm clock that fell off the bedside table. I crawl as far as the headphone wire will allow. I pull open a drawer and put on whatever I can find. I'm shaking, my teeth are clattering uncontrollably. It always happens this way. Every time.

Every time I reincarnate.

I hear the bells, too, every time. Each time they ring harder and louder than before. Like now. They crash against the wall of music inside my head. The music doesn't really help anymore, not even when I shove the headphones up against my ears, not even when I scream until my throat is raw. I have to leave: I get up and run out of the room, down the stairs and into the street with my headphones on, the music throbbing and the infernal bells ringing. Ringing for the dead and ringing for me.

Il Gabinetto Regionale di Polizia Scientifica della Questura di Bologna is housed in a renovated seventeenth-century convent. In the entrance, printed on the wall above the sweeping, central staircase, is an enlarged reproduction of Leonardo da Vinci's *Vitruvian Man*. They were late. Grazia hurried up the stairs. Suddenly she stopped, curbed by the same dull pain that she had felt in her abdomen earlier that morning. A look of irritation crossed her face.

"Shit," she whispered to herself, but Vittorio heard her anyway.

"What's the matter?" he asked.

"Nothing."

She unzipped her bomber jacket and reached inside to shift the position of her gun, which she kept in a holster clipped to her belt. She moved the holster back onto her hip, then forward again. The feeling didn't go away.

"I hope you're not getting sick," Vittorio said, looping his arm through hers, his fingers pressing against the rough olive fabric of her coat. "I need you with me at a hundred percent. I've got to convince them."

"Don't worry, I'll be fine."

"You know the material better than anyone and if you don't feel well . . ."

"Don't worry. I'll be fine."

"It's not the flu, is it? They say there's a nasty flu going around."

"Look, Vittorio, I'm about to get my period, OK? It always happens like this. Don't worry. It's normal."

"Oh," he said with some embarrassment and loosened his hold on her arm. By the time he went to renew his grasp on her she had already slipped out of his hold and was running up the stairs two by two. Vittorio hurried to catch up and followed her as she walked briskly down the long hall.

"I know it's normal, Grazia," he said. "You're a woman."

"I'm a cop."

"All right, you're a cop. But so am I. And I want to make sure we get this case. You know which pictures to show — and when?"

Grazia nodded. She shut her eyes and visualized the long list of files, the toolbar next to the column of names, the black arrow that made them scroll up and down. She could click on them and open them in her mind. Names, dates, and images.

"I know what to do."

"And the grand finale?"

"That too."

"Which one is it?"

"Catia."

CATIA001.jpg. She blinked. She could see the black square at the top of the screen, the words highlighted in green. If she clicked on the writing the square would open and the picture would appear. Grazia blinked to clear her vision. Then she tried not to blink at all. She tried to forget about Catia.

"Okay, sweetheart," Vittorio said, "I want you to know what we're up against here. You've never had to deal with these guys before. They're tough. The hardest one to convince is the questore, the chief of police. The assistant public prosecutor, Procuratore Alvau, is young and doesn't have a lot of experience; he might even like the idea of getting some good publicity out of a case like this. The questore is the complete opposite. He detests any kind of scandal and will never admit that his city has problems. He'd also have to take the heat for mishandling things up until now. He even had the head of forensics transferred out so we wouldn't have anyone to lean on—but we know how to get him, don't we? Are you ready, sweetheart?"

Grazia didn't reply. She gave him a sidelong look, then frowned and shoved her hands deep into the pockets of her jacket. She stopped in front of a low, narrow doorway that had the words IERONIMUS FRATER, MDCLXXIII carved in long, thin letters into the heavy keystone. Vittorio straightened his tie and tugged at the cuffs of his overcoat. He lowered his head so he wouldn't bump it and turned to Grazia one last time.

"Okay, Ispettore Negro, let's get their ass." Then, as he walked through the doorway, he called out, "Hello? May we come in? Sorry about the delay . . . an accident on the freeway."

The laboratory for special investigations was created by joining together two monks' cells. It has stone walls, beamed ceilings, and several small windows, encased by large, roughly hewn stones. The floor is tiled with terracotta. The beams are painted black. If there were an altar, a crucifix, and a candelabra, it would resemble a monastery chapel. Instead, a computer terminal, its monitor, modem, and keyboard, together with a five-screen television security system, long coils of cables, and an assortment of plugs make of the room headquarters for forensics.

The screensaver on the computer read POLIZIA DI STATO in cubic lettering; the words rotated furiously around a central focal point, seeming at first close and then far away, gigantic and then miniscule. Two men stood in front of one of the color television screens with a camera on a tripod, taking pictures of a videotaped student protest. They had paused the video on an image of a young man with a black kaffiyeh around his neck. Perched on a stool next to the computer sat the procuratore. He wore a navy blue overcoat and kept his hands in his pockets. He looked like a dark, curved crow. The questore sat in a chair next to the two men with the camera.

"Aha, finally," the questore said as Vittorio walked into the room. Then, tapping one of the two men on the shoulder, he said, "Enough for now, boys." To the dark blue crow he announced emphatically, "The Americans have landed! USC is here."

To Grazia the questore seemed like the kind of man who combed his hair in a way that would make him look taller. The blue crow, on the other hand, had a young face and blond hair, a lock of which fell across his forehead and over his red tortoiseshell glasses. Vittorio looked the same as ever: slightly tan, elegantly dressed, hair combed back, a sincere expression on his face, right hand extended in greeting. He looked more like an executive at a business meeting than a criminologist with a degree in psychiatry, the brightest and youngest supervisor of a forensics unit, they said.

"How do you do; I'm Commissario Capo Vittorio Poletto and this is Ispettore Negro. And if you don't mind, sir, it's actually UASC."

"Excuse me," Procuratore Alvau interjected, "but would someone mind telling me just what the hell UASC stands for?"

"Unit for the Analysis of Serial Crimes. We're called in on cases with possible *assassini seriali,* sort of like the VICAP unit of the FBI."

"Now hold on, Dottor Poletto, this is Italy, not the United States—"

"Of course, Signor Questore. In fact, our team is significantly different from theirs; we're an integral part of the forensic unit."

Grazia noticed how delicately Vittorio had made his point. He had deliberately used the Italian *assassini seriali,* instead of the widely accepted American phrase, "serial killers." He didn't want to risk losing the case by seeming overzealous. She wanted to smile, but her cramps held her back. The assistant procuratore shifted his position on the stool, extending one leg and pulling his coat tightly around himself.

"So, you think there might be an *assassino seriale* here in Bologna?"

Grazia turned to look at Vittorio. He nodded slowly, frowning, his lips pressed tightly together. He looked resolute.

"Yes, Dottor Alvau, we believe there is."

He said it so compellingly that even the questore was left speechless. Vittorio took advantage of their silence.

"I'd like you both to have a look at something, if you wouldn't mind waiting while we hook up to SCIPS—"

"More damn acronyms . . ."

"Sorry, Dottor Alvau, professional hazard. SCIPS is the unit that deals with the computer systems of forensics. Grazia—would you come to the computer, please."

Grazia quickly walked over to the terminal and sat down in front of the screen. When she moved the mouse, the rotating words vanished, but it must have been dusty, because the cursor moved unevenly across the screen. Grazia had to maneuver it forcefully to make the arrow point to the yellow trumpet icon. If there had been complete silence in the room they would have been able to hear the program starting up and the modem dialing, but Vittorio kept talking. He didn't want to give the procuratore a minute to think.

"So, Dottor Alvau, UASC was started in December 1995. Our head office is in Rome, where we work in tandem with the mobile unit of the police that investigates 'homicides with no apparent motive and serial carnal violence.' One of our many functions is to provide what we call 'Preventive Counseling.'"

"Ha!" the questore let out a loud, sarcastic laugh. He would have continued but when the computer screen suddenly turned bright blue, he shut his mouth in respectful silence.

"This program is called SACS. It deals with the systemic analysis of crime scenes. It processes data gathered by SART, an operating system that houses circumstantial data stored in SCIPS. The program automatically pools together data and information from different cases and highlights the connections between them—we call it the Killer Catcher."

Big mistake. The questore started to laugh again, this time directing his amusement at the computer. He laughed hard, as if the "Killer Catcher" were the name of a cartoon show. Alvau, however, solemnly raised his hand as if to silence the laughter, adjusted his eyeglasses, and looked closely at the screen.

"And what exactly have you discovered?"

His composure regained, Vittorio lowered his hand onto Grazia's shoulder. Presenting a serious expression, he caressed the scratchy material of her bomber jacket.

"Please, Ispettore Negro, you may proceed."

Grazia felt all eyes on her. The questore was looking over her shoulder, his breath on her ear. Before, when he had laughed, she had felt a warm, hard fleck of his saliva hit her on the cheek. The assistant procuratore loomed like a vulture behind her. Vittorio's warm hand was still on her shoulder, the tip of his finger pressing her collarbone. Her stomach ached; she felt pressure in her kidneys, along her back and into the bones of her legs, which she kept crossed under the table. Under her padded jacket and sweatshirt, under her thin cotton camisole, her breasts felt heavy and sore. *Shit.* Her thoughts went to the container of tampons in her jacket pocket next to the spare Beretta cartridge clip. She took a deep breath, cleared her throat, and clicked open the files, one by one.

"Graziano case: Bologna, December 1994. University student. From Palermo. Twenty-five years old. Single occupant of a studio apartment in the Hills.

"Lucchesi case: San Lazzaro di Bologna, November 1995. Part-time, returning university student. Originally from Genova. Twenty-eight years old. Junkie. Previous arrests for theft and drug trafficking.

"Farolfi–Baldi case: Castenaso di Bologna, May '96. A couple. Both students. Both from Napoli. Made a living by subletting apartments to other nonlocals. Dog owners. The dog was killed too."

Grazia took a breath. *Don't mention the murders,* Vittorio had said. Just open the files, show the witness reports, the records, the pictures of the victims—*but alive, not dead.* Grazia went through the entire collection: the completed police forms, the paperwork done by various Carabinieri and squadra mobile agents, the victims' blurry ID pictures or overexposed photographs of them at the beach, standing on a pier, looking out to sea. Save the best for last, Vittorio had told her. The best.

CATIA001.jpg. Grazia tried not to think about it.

"The Assirelli–Assirelli–Assirelli–Fierro case: December 1996."

This time there were two squares, *ASS1.JPG* and *ASS2.JPG*. Grazia moved the mouse until the cursor pointed to *ASS1* and clicked twice. A photograph of a family appeared. Father, mother, son, and daughter were at a table in some kind of trattoria celebrating a birthday or New Year's Eve.

"They lived in Coriano di Rimini, in the hills, in an isolated villa. These people had children."

ASS2. Double-click. This picture showed the same table at the trattoria, the same colorful wooden wheel hanging on the wall, the same fireplace and mantle with the same straw-covered souvenir bottle on it. The only difference was that in the second picture the Assirelli family was absent. There was something disconcerting about the rumpled tablecloth, the way a section of the table was bare. A dark stain ran down the wall and under the table, along the floor and out the door at the far end of the image. Alvau leaned forward to get a better look, as though he wanted to follow that blotchy mark with his gaze. Grazia thought better of pushing him back with her shoulders.

"But all these cases were closed," the questore said with some hesitation.

"Nobody was ever charged," Grazia said. "They said the student from Palermo was mixed up with a gay crowd, the San Lazzaro police think the junkie was tied into a drug deal. The Castenaso couple . . ."

"I remember," Alvau interjected. "Murder One, committed during the course of robbery. No one was ever incriminated. "

The questore spoke up. "As for the Assirelli family, the Procura di Rimini still wants to question that gypsy, the one who's in prison in the former Yugoslavia now for having killed a family in Pavia. It all seems quite logical to me. I can't see anything that links the cases together."

"Neither can I," said Alvau, "Nothing at all. I can't imagine how there could be . . . and yet there's . . . Ispettore Negro, are you all right?"

Her cramps had made Grazia move suddenly.

"Is something wrong?" the questore asked.

"No, no, I'm fine," Grazia replied, shaking her head.

"Ispettore Negro is . . ." Vittorio began to explain.

"It's the flu," said Alvau firmly. "I have it too. It's awful."

"No, no . . ."

"Ispettore Negro is . . ."

"I noticed right away how pale the signorina was. Right away."

"Can you believe the flu this year! Three different viruses! It goes right to your stomach . . ."

"No, really . . ."

"Ispettore Negro is . . ."

"Maybe we should go into the other room, so she can . . ."

"Ispettore Negro is—um—slightly indisposed."

"Oh," Alvau and the questore both said.

Grazia's cheeks turned bright red.

"There *are* connections between the murders," she said brusquely. "First of all, the M.O. is always the same:

a bestial force massacres everything in its path. Pure violence. No sex, no fetishism, nothing. Just pure violence."

"M.O: Modus Operandi," Vittorio whispered to Alvau.

"I know, I know," he said, nodding vehemently.

"Second: in each case at least one victim is stripped of his clothing and left naked. The boy from Palermo, the junkie, Andrea Farolfi, and Maurizio Assirelli, the son of the family from Coriano. Naked—head to toe."

"Well, that's not so strange . . ." the questore said but no one seemed to be listening to him.

"Third: all the victims are students. Kids from the university."

The questore slammed his fist down on the table so hard that everyone turned to look at him.

"Someone murdering students! Absurd! I won't hear of it." He reached out and grabbed Alvau's arm in rage. "Do you realize what this would mean? Do you have any idea? There are two hundred thousand students in this city. Do you know what would happen if the news gets out that there's a maniac on the loose killing students? Here? In Bologna, of all places? It's absurd!"

Vittorio reached out and took hold of Alvau's other arm. "Listen to me, Dottor Alvau, we have precise statistics that show . . ."

"Now just a second, Dottor Poletto," the questore said, grabbing Vittorio's wrist with his free hand. "These 'precise statistics' of yours . . ."

"Would you listen to me, Signor Questore . . ."

"No, let me finish . . ."

Grazia sat up straight, trapped by a reticulum of arms and hands. She would have liked to stun them all by getting to her feet but she remembered CATIA001.jpg waiting silently in a far corner of the screen.

CATIA001.jpg.

Grazia moved the arrow onto the icon, then clicked and dragged it into the middle of the screen.

CATIA001.jpg.

She spoke up. "Dottor Alvau, I think we have at least one good reason to pursue this investigation."

CATIA001.jpg.

"Oh, really? And what on earth might that be?" he asked.

"To prevent this from ever happening again," she said and clicked twice. A picture appeared on the screen. It was of Catia Assirelli, age eleven, as taken by a photographer from forensics on December 21, 1996, at 3:32 P.M.

"Oh my God!" the assistant procuratore exclaimed, turning away. "Oh my God . . . no!"

In a habitual gesture, Vittorio rapidly extended his arm, then bent it toward him to check his wristwatch, which was hidden under the sleeve of his overcoat.

"Shit. It's late," he said, one hand on the roof of the blue- and-white police car and one foot inside it. The driver was gunning the motor. "I can't miss the Pendolino."

"Don't worry, you'll catch it," Grazia murmured. She watched him settle into the car and waited until he had folded his raincoat across his lap before firmly shutting the door behind him. Vittorio lowered the window.

"It looks like we did it. At least Alvau has decided to give us the case for a while, despite that shithead of a questore. Nice job with the picture of the girl at the end. A bit risky, but worth it. Well done, sweetheart."

Grazia smiled but didn't look at him. She stared at the asphalt. She felt a damp, heavy weight inside her, both in her abdomen and farther up, near her heart. Her throat tickled. She thought she might cry. Vittorio leaned out the window and squeezed her arm.

"I don't need to remind you how important this project is to UASC. We've invested a lot in it and expect the best from you. I expect the best from you. You're our man in the field. I trust that fierce, animal instinct in you that I like so much. Use it. Get him. *Bacio*."

Grazia bent down and skimmed Vittorio's cheek with a light kiss, the way a child would. Vittorio withdrew into the car, turned to the officer in the driver's seat, patted him on the arm, and said, "If I miss that train, I'll have you transferred to Sardinia." Then, as they were pulling out, he turned to Grazia and added, "Call me on my cell phone whenever you need to."

Grazia slowly extracted her hand from her pocket to wave good-bye. Then she zipped her jacket up to her chin. The evening air had turned cold and gray. Suddenly, the parking lot in Piazza Roosevelt seemed larger than before, as if it had expanded around her. As if Bologna itself had become an immense and infinitely dilating city. She stood there, her hands deep in the pockets of her bomber jacket, the need to cry spreading slowly across her face.

"Fuck you," she said, wiping away the single tear that she had not been able to hold back. PMS, she thought to herself. Then, as she was walking back through the porticoes to headquarters, she whispered it again for good measure.

".Fuck you."

Sometimes my mother comes upstairs to see what I'm doing.

The sound of her slippers on the stairs is like light breathing, with no beginning or end. I hear her instantly. The creak of the wooden steps. The gentle tap of her wedding band on the brass railing, metal on metal. When she stops halfway up to catch her breath, her breathing sounds wide and short; the stairs that lead to my room are narrow and steep.

When I hear her — if I hear her in time — I lie down on the sofa and pretend to be asleep. I lie very still. The door handle rasps open, like the sound of someone clearing their throat. Her slippers brush over the threshold, she says "ssshhhh" to herself. Then I hear the handle again, the breathing sound of her slippers as she retreats downstairs, the creak of the steps, the tap of her ring, until I can't hear anything anymore. The first few times, when I'd lie down without even pulling the plaid blanket over myself, she would come and cover me with it. Sometimes she notices that I'm not really sleeping.

"Are you asleep?" she says.

And she starts talking.

If I stay in my swivel chair and pretend to be asleep, either by leaning all the way back with my head on the headrest or all the way forward with my arms crossed in front of me like a pretzel, it never works. She comes up to me, taps me on the shoulder and says, "You should go to bed if you're tired."

And then she starts talking.

But if I have all my scanners and the music on, there's no way out. She hears them from downstairs and knows I'm not sleeping. The only thing to do then is to turn the dial to a different frequency, tune in to a chat room, and listen to the conversations on the Internet.

I've only recently figured out how to do this. Modems send each other signals through the telephone lines with irregular rings. Even though the signals get distorted by electrical currents, you can still pick up the messages. I hear a lot of them while I'm combing the airwaves with the scanner. It sounds like a volley of modified whistles. Or like a flock of small birds making chirpy yellow sounds over gusts of blue, frizzy wind. I had heard them before but it only recently occurred to me that I could hook up the signals to the audio function of my computer. The whistles become voices and the voices come out of my speakers in low, flat, artificial tones. I can't pick up data but when messages are being exchanged in chat rooms, I hear words. Words that get typed by people on their keyboards; words that appear on other people's screens; words that get translated into voices. Voices of the city. They read each other. I listen to them.

My mother hates the voice synthesizer of my computer.

"Oh God, that thing . . . I can't stand it," she says, and leaves. That's why I turn it on as soon as I hear her coming. But sometimes she stays anyway.

And she starts talking.

"God, that thing . . . I can't stand it. What are you doing? What are you listening to? Isn't the music too loud? Your ears are delicate, you know."

I don't listen to Chet Baker during the day. "Almost Blue" is night music. During the day I listen to the radio or put on a CD. There's a program I like called *Barfly*. It comes on in the afternoon. They only play jazz. There's no talking. Only a few ads. Just jazz. Mostly be-bop.

Coleman Hawkins.

A throbbing, purple saxophone. Warmth. The piano, the bass, and the drums melt into each other. They become invisible and he passes right through them.

My mother's voice sounds green because of the cigarette she just smoked. I can smell her coming—smoke and the smell of hairspray that she uses on her wig. She speaks with the cadence of mountain people—her vowel sounds rise and fall openly, sustaining the syllables. It's almost as if she's singing.

"I don't know why you didn't study the piano when you were in school. You'd be a musician by now, instead of being up here listening to that godawful thing. God, that thing. I can't stand it."

The voice synthesizer always sounds the same. It doesn't have any inflection, it doesn't breathe, it has no color. It has a male voice. It trills its *R*s slightly and sometimes it seems to prolong the vowel sounds. It doesn't pause between words. Sometimes it pauses between one person's sentences and another's.

— hi comma my name is rita comma where are you writing from question mark —

— from bologna comma and you question mark —

— me too period what sign are you question mark —

— scorpio what about you question mark —

The sound of the synthesizer, the music, and my mother's voice bleed into each other. Together, they sound like an instrument being played off-time.

Miles Davis. Round, red, airy trumpet sounds blow straight through my mother's words.

"Even the private tutor that used to come here after you stopped going to school used to say 'touch things, feel them, use your fingers.'"

With a plunger mute he flattens the trumpet sound, then widens it. It's as if the music were made of gauze and the voice from the synthesizer gets wrapped inside it.

— aquarius comma ascendant cancer comma moon in sagittarius period —

— that's beautiful Rita comma really beautiful period —

— why hyphen you know about horoscopes question mark —

"She was a sweet lady, that tutor. Too bad you didn't want her to come over any more. The one after her wasn't as nice, I agree with you on that. I don't think she cared as much about her work . . ."

Then he plays the trumpet without the mute and the sound blows beautiful, yellow holes through everything.

"I mean, I don't want to force you, but if you went out now and then it might be good for you."

—you're just like me comma Rita comma only one thing frightens us period—

—what question mark—

—solitude period—

A long, purple note glides out of Miles Davis's trumpet, drizzles down, and then dies out. My mother and the synthesizer prolong the finale.

"It was different when your father was alive."

—Yes comma solitude period—

Ron Carter: a twisted, discordant bass comes at you from nowhere. Usually it's a beautiful, bluish shade of purple, but today, mixed with the voice synthesizer, it turns green. I'm just about to turn the dial, when I hear:

—do you have a microphone question mark—

—yes—

I keep the scanner where it is but turn down the volume.

"Hi. Can you hear me?" she asks.

A young woman. Her "Hi" sounds more like "Hey" or "Haigh." She's nervous. Anxious.

"A little . . . wait, let me try and . . . how's this?"

A man. Young. Something in his voice doesn't sound right. I don't like it.

She smiles. I can hear it in the way her words extend across her mouth. She's breathing through her vowels with a reddish glow. Ironic. Playful. Excited.

"Do you know how to use the mike or not? I mean, is this your computer or did you steal it? Just joking . . . I know Scorpios can get pretty touchy."

"Not me. I'm totally mellow. I'm a Scorpio in one way only."

"How?"

"Guess."

I don't like him. His voice is green. It sidles up to the distorted bass playing softly in the background, pushing it back like a flap of skin. His voice is green because it has no color. Color comes from the way a person breathes through their words. From the pressure of their breath. If the pressure is low, they're sad, anxious, or needy. If the pressure is high, they're sincere, ironic, or good-natured. If the pressure is even, they're either indifferent or conclusive. If the pressure increases all of a sudden, they're threatening, vulgar, or violent. If the pressure fluctuates and gets rounded out on the corners, then they're being affectionate, malicious, or sensual. This voice is none of these. It's only slightly stronger than the voice of the synthesizer, only slightly fuller. It's a fake, green voice.

"Listen, Scorpio, you're not going to start talking about sex, are you? I mean you're not one of those people that goes on-line to pick up girls, I hope . . ."

"No way, not at all."

Low pressure. Extremely low pressure. Too low. Afflicted. Beaten. Shattered.

"No, I meant that I'm a Scorpio in the way I distance myself from people. The way a scorpion hides under rocks. I'm always ready to defend myself from everything and everybody. I sting so as not to get stung. Sometimes I feel alone, though. Like now."

"Sorry, Scorpio, I didn't mean to . . . I know what you mean. Sometimes I feel lonely too."

She fell for it. Her voice softened. The pressure on the vowel sounds went down in a convinced sigh. I know exactly how things will go from here: how old are you, what music do you listen to, what do you like to do, where can we meet . . .

"So what kind of music do you listen to, Scorpio?"

"You mean, right now?"

"Why, are you listening to something? I can't hear anything."

"I have my Walkman on, but I can still hear you."

I can't stand the green voice. There's something about it that sends shivers up my spine. It's as if there's another sound inside it. Under it. As if something was being mumbled in the silences, like a prayer, but it's not a prayer. It's whispering something.

Bells clanging.

"What do you do, Scorpio? I go to DAMS, the art school. I do Bhutan dance, origami, and I'm learning shiatsu."

"I don't know. Hey Rita . . . do you believe in reincarnation?"

His voice is flat, but I hear something moving under it. Something that puffs up and then deflates with a hiss. And whispering.

Clanging, clanging, clanging.

It scares me.

"Hey Rita . . . you think we can get together some-time?"

I turn the dial with a flick of my thumb. The scanner crackles over dark silence. I realize that my mother's voice is no longer present. And that *Barfly* is over. I don't like the kind of music they're playing now. I can still hear that voice inside my head. It sends shivers up my spine, like when I was younger and wore braces and would rub the bands together. To forget about that cold feeling I turn on my stereo and turn up the volume.

"Almost Blue."

Just as the bass begins to resonate, an instant before Chet Baker starts to sing, the scanner stops searching. I hear her voice.

A blue voice.

"Hello, Vittorio? It's me, Grazia. No, everything is fine. I just wanted to . . . yes, no, the questore's not a problem. Sure, I'll be all right. Sure."

He's not listening to her. He's a black pause, empty silence. He's talking on a GSM, the kind you can't inter-cept. Or he could be on a house phone, but they have a different, pinker, kind of silence.

"No, really, I'm fine. They've given me two men from the mobile unit. They'll let me know if . . . of course I'm working on it. Don't worry, Vittorio, I'll take care of it."

Can't he tell she's crying? Can't he hear the wetness in her voice? She's holding back the words so that they don't slip away from her, like when you're walking on a wet surface. She breathes the words across her lips, just like Chet Baker does. Her eyes are definitely closed.

"Vittorio? Can you hold on for a second? One of the officers is signaling me . . ."

She places a hand over the microphone. I can tell by the way it gets fuzzy. I lean my head against the speakers so that I'll be closer to her when she comes back to the phone.

I like her voice. It's a soft voice. Young, a little sad. There's a bit of South in her voice. Low and warm. Round. Full. Violet, with red highlights.

The bluest voice I've ever heard.

But when she comes back to the phone, her voice has changed. She's not crying anymore. She sounds tough. She's speaking so quickly that I barely recognize her.

"Vittorio? I'll call you back. They've found another one."

Hey Rita . . . do you believe in reincarnation?

"Watch out, signorina . . . most of the blood's dry now, but there's still some on the ceiling that drips down occasionally."

Grazia was sorry she'd changed out of her jeans, not only because of this bloated feeling, which she knew was partially her imagination, but because nobody took her for a police officer. In her short, gray wool dress, black stockings, and laced-up combat boots, Grazia looked more like a woman than usual. Despite her bomber jacket and the Polizia di Stato ID tag, they assumed she was either a student or a journalist. Perhaps it was because the only officers in the devastated apartment were from the Carabinieri Corps, and they were all armed and in military uniform. Perhaps it was because she was the only woman present.

"Fuck," she said to herself, taking a deep breath even though she wasn't wearing a protective mask.

The boy had been dead for a week when they found him. The stench had led to his discovery. The landlady, who hadn't seen him for several days, had rung his doorbell in the morning but no one had answered. Later, on her way back upstairs that afternoon, she noticed his door was ajar. She also noticed a strong, pungent odor, as if someone had been boiling jam for hours. The stench of death.

One room, a bathroom, and a kitchen counter. That's all. A typical apartment for a student.

The brigadiere was tall and polite. He took off his mask to talk to her but put it right back on again, unable to hide his nausea. Grazia swallowed and clenched her teeth. She frowned.

"What condition was the corpse in?" she asked.

"He was a mess, signorina. It was awful. The coroner said that he was about twenty. It could have been Paolo Miserocchi, the kid that rented the apartment. Luckily, they've already taken away the body."

"I mean—was he clothed or naked? And please don't call me signorina."

"Sorry, I had no idea. You seem awfully young to be married. But you're right, signorina isn't even legally correct anymore. "

"Ispettore Negro, if you don't mind. I'm not a signora, I'm a colleague. You can call me Ispettore."

Behind his mask, the brigadiere blushed. He looked her over. She stood on the tips of her toes to see what was on the top bunk, her hands behind her back. She was careful not to touch anything, which was hard to do. The floor was strewn with pieces of glass, books, clothes, CDs, pieces of a broken wooden mask. The closet doors had been flung open and all the drawers pulled out. The bedside table had fallen over. Posters had been torn off the wall — one of Pamela Anderson lay crumpled in a corner. The chair, desk, and computer, however, were in order. And clean.

"Obviously, he was naked," the brigadiere said. "The bulletin said to inform you if we found a naked victim. That's why you're here. Ispettore."

Grazia delicately stepped over the rubble to get closer to the desk. She stuck her hands in her jacket pockets and reached round to rub her lower back. No relief. She leaned down to the keyboard and sniffed. She could detect the acrid odor of the fingerprinting dust. She barely noticed the smell of death anymore.

"I'd like to see the fingerprints as soon as possible, please," she said.

"Don't worry, you won't find ours among them," the brigadiere replied. "The guard that turned off the computer was wearing . . ."

Grazia turned to look at him.

"You saved everything before turning it off, naturally," she said.

"Obviously," the brigadiere replied but only after an instant's hesitation. He looked apprehensive and spoke cautiously, his smile frozen beneath his mask.

"Shit," Grazia murmured. The brigadiere could see the anger in her eyes and blushed again.

"I'd like to speak with the officer who turned off the computer," Grazia said. "Can you call him over, please?" It wasn't so much of a question as an order. The brigadiere nodded and stood to attention, his arms by his sides, hands on the red stripes of his uniform trousers.

"Of course—by all means—Canavese! Over here, immediately!"

Canavese was standing next to the only open window in the apartment, taking deep breaths of fresh air. He stepped away from the window with an irritated expression but when he saw Grazia standing next to the brigadiere, it vanished. His eyes wandered over her body, across her breasts, up her legs, and to her mouth. He strode forward in his tall, shiny boots, his white bandolier and holster swinging. He, too, was tall.

"Journalist?" he asked, then noticed the ID around her neck. "Aha—a cousin. Cute, too. Much better than our own colleagues, wouldn't you say, brigadiere? I always said that the police . . ."

Grazia glared at him. She noticed that Canavese was standing on a piece of paper streaked in half with red. On his way over to her from the window, he had audaciously marched across everything that had come underfoot. Grazia sighed and shook her head. She decided not to bother asking if he had saved anything before turning off the computer.

"Do you remember what was written on the screen? Was it a document? A program? Do you remember anything it said?"

Canavese shrugged and shook his head.

"I don't know too much about computers," he said. "It was all black. There was colored writing that moved across it . . . but I didn't stop to read it."

"Everything can be retrieved," the brigadiere spoke up. "Our computer specialists are amazing."

"It doesn't matter," Grazia mumbled. "That was just a screensaver—something that comes up during the long pauses to . . . well, it doesn't really matter."

"As soon as I touched the desk, it disappeared," Canavese said, sticking one finger under his beret and scratching his head. "Wait a minute . . . the, ummm, what do you call it?"

"The screen," Grazia offered.

"Yeah, that's it." Canavese ran his hand along the gentle curve of the monitor. The brigadiere made a move to stop him, but Grazia glared at him, indicating him to let the officer finish his thought. "The screen was divided in two by a blue line. There was a yellow square on top and a yellow square on the bottom and there was writing on both of them."

"A chat room!" Grazia exclaimed. "He was in a chat room with someone. Well done. Congratulations."

"Thank you," Canavese said naively.

"Anyway, our computer guys really can work miracles, Ispettore," the brigadiere said. "And besides, didn't it happen to you guys too? Remember the Via Poma case? When the police turned off the computer . . ."

"Yes, I remember." Grazia cut him short. "I suppose that makes us even. I'd like to speak to the woman who found the corpse, please."

Anna Bulzamini Lazzaroni—you know, like the *biscotti* company? you can write that down, Signorina—lived across the hall. She was standing in the entrance of her apartment with a capitano from the carabinieri. This man was taller than both Canavese and the brigadiere. At first he wouldn't let Grazia in. No journalists allowed, sorry. Oh, you're with the police? Fine. You're the serial killer specialist? Are you sure? We think it's drug related. Miserocchi was selling Ecstasy to the whole damn business school.

"Anna Bulzamini Lazzaroni — you know, like the biscotti company? you can write that down, Signorina. Well, not the biscotti family, but we're related.

"Yes, I rent out apartments to students from the university, but believe you me, it's not the nicest line of work to be in. More than anything else, it's a constant quarrel. The last time I saw Paolo, the boy across the hall, was about a week ago. I heard him on the landing so I went to tell him that his rent was due but he never brought it to me, so I rang his bell but he wasn't there, so then I went back and rang again but he still didn't answer. No, I never thought anything had happened to him. I suppose because the next day he was there. Well, it wasn't really him, I guess. I mean it was a friend of his who said that Paolo wasn't there. Sure I saw the friend. I even invited him over for a cup of coffee — you know how these guys sublet their places when they go away for a while — I don't like that, so I wanted to be sure . . . No, I had never seen him before but I couldn't exactly ask for his ID, now could I? Well, let's see. What was he like? Like all the others, I guess. A normal student, from the university. He had a round face, dark skin, long side-burns which were shaved to a point, and one of those little goatees that everyone's wearing these days. He was kind and had good manners (even though he kept his headphones on the whole time he was here and I didn't like that very much, no). He wouldn't stop touching my collection of little glass animals—I thought to myself, better keep an eye on this guy or he's going to steal something. But I checked after he left and everything was there. Anyway, I wanted my rent money. It doesn't grow on trees, right? So I called every day but the line was always busy. I thought, I bet that guy is going to skip out of here and leave me a huge phone bill or something. A couple of times the friend answered the phone but today the line was always busy so I went over to ring the bell but the door was open—and it smelled terrible. Oh God, I have to sit down or I'll be sick."

Anna Bulzamini Lazzaroni leaned heavily on the capitano's arm. He guided her to an armchair in the living room. Grazia examined the miniature glass figurines lined up on the highboy. She saw an elephant, a duck, a puppy . . . all of them covered with a light veil of fingerprinting dust. It looked as though a light, gray snow had suddenly fallen from above.

"That fierce, animal instinct," Vittorio had said.

That instinct.

Grazia picked up a small crocodile by its tail so as not to smudge the fingerprints and quickly slipped it into her pocket just as the capitano turned toward her. She pulled her hand out of her pocket so quickly, she spilled all of its contents to the floor: photographs of the homicide victims, her spare cartridge, the tampon container, and even the crocodile, which bounced onto a corner of the carpet. Flustered, she knelt down to gather it up,

looking over to see if the capitano had noticed the crocodile. His gaze, however, had been distracted by the tampon holder, which had landed between his shiny black
boots. He picked it up and handed it back to her with a
slight tap of his heels and a gentle smile. Grazia stuffed it
back into her pocket along with the photographs.

"Excuse me, signorina," Anna Bulzamini Lazzaroni
said, "May I see what you've got in your pocket?"

Grazia blushed, unsure what to do. She looked at the
capitano in surprise. He looked back at her, similarly
perplexed, almost suspicious. Anna Bulzamini Lazzaroni
leaned forward and pointed.

"That! There, sticking out of your pocket. What is
that? A photograph?"

"Yes," Grazia mumbled, confused, extracting the pictures from her pocket, "Yes, they're pictures of . . ." and
she tried to explain.

"Can I see them?" Anna Bulzamini asked. The capitano, without hesitating, plucked them out of Grazia's
grasp and handed them to the widow with another
slight tap of his heels.

"That's him!"

"Who?" Grazia and the capitano both asked.

"The boy with headphones. The one that was stay-
ing at Paolo's. I'd recognize him anywhere. That's him,
I'm sure of it."

Grazia breathed in sharply. A shiver crept up her
back to the nape of her neck. The photograph that
Anna Bulzamini Lazzaroni held up was of a boy with a
round face, dark skin, long sideburns shaved to a point,

and one of those little goatees that everyone's wearing these days.

It was the color print of *ASS3.jpg*.

Maurizio Assirelli.

Murdered in Coriano di Rimini on December 21, 1996.

Sometimes I feel thousands of tiny fishhooks under my skin, clawing at my face, pulling it into my throat. They come from somewhere under my tongue and explode through my head like shooting stars. I feel the barbs pulling at my pores, tugging so delicately they barely even seem to pierce the skin. I like to look in a mirror when it happens. My face gets all shiny, as if covered with millions of microscopic silver drops. Infinitesimal, luminous dots. But then, when the hooks pull hard and my whole face crinkles up from the inside, like a fist closing around itself, then I feel my eyes, nose, lips, cheeks, and hair getting shoved down my throat.

Sometimes my shadow is darker than other people's. I've seen it. Sometimes, when I'm walking along the street, it stains the wall alongside me. It leaves a mark on the street signs and advertisements, on the cement walls. It gets thick and dark. Sometimes I get scared that someone will notice it but I can't run away from it because it would follow me. It would spread out, sticky and black, alongside me. That's why I stay close to the wall.

Sometimes I feel something slithering under my skin, some kind of animal. I don't know exactly what because it always stays under the surface. But if I pull up my sleeve fast enough, I see a small, hard bump move up my arm to my shoulder, as if it wants to get away. When I take off my shirt, I can see it move across my chest and down to my stomach. Then it travels up again. It's like a lumpy mass that crawls forward by scrunching up, then extending itself again. Inchworming. It itches but I can't do anything about it. Once I cut into my skin as it was creeping up my arm. I saw something stick out — a small green comma. I tried to pull it out but it slipped away. I think it had scales. It prickled. I had to let go. It went back in.

Sometimes these things happen to me.

Sometimes.

But I always — always, always, always — hear the evil death bells inside my head. They ring constantly. They're ringing for me.

Sometimes I feel something slithering under my skin, some kind of animal, but I don't know what it is.

"It's not a crocodile . . . it's some kind of a lizard."

"It looks like a dragon to me, with that crest."

"No, it's a salamander. Salamanders are long like that."

"Excuse me, can we continue with the procedure now?"

The forensic lab technician looked over at Ispettore Matera and smiled tacitly. He wiped his hands on his lab coat and proceeded to pick up the glass statuette with a pair of tweezers. Then, with a quick glance at Sovrintendente Sarrina, he put the crocodile, lizard, salamander, or whatever it was into the oven chamber. He regulated the thermostat and turned on the appliance. Sarrina watched Grazia out of the corner of his eye, tapping a fingernail against his front tooth.

"Would you mind not doing that?" Grazia said, annoyed at having to ask. Her gaze was fixed on the vapors of cyanoacrylate that were filling the chamber with a white mist, as if someone were on the inside, breathing on the glass.

"Sorry," Sarrina said, but it was clear from his voice that he was smiling.

At the Bologna Questura Forensic Unit, all fingerprints are processed and stored in a cavernous room,
lined floor to ceiling with electronically programmed
and digitalized filing cabinets. The rows of cabinets
have been neatly positioned between the thick stone
columns and under the vaulted arches of the renovated
convent. Being in the room gives one the opposite
effect of looking at a dinosaur in a museum: The cabinets are like the skeleton of some modern animal inside
a prehistoric room.

Grazia leaned against the cabinets, her hands in the
pockets of her unzipped jacket against her aching
abdomen. She watched as the vapors of cyanoacrylate
settled on the statuette, reacting with the fat and sweat
particles present in the fingerprints, detailing the back
of the figurine with diaphanous circles.

"Be careful," she whispered as the technician extracted
the chimerical animal from the chamber and placed it
under the microscope to photograph it. Matera and
Sarrina, the two men assigned to Grazia by the questore,
observed from a distance. Sarrina was sitting on the edge
of the table, an ironic smile on his face. Matera was sitting on a chair. Though he seemed more fatherly and
patient than Sarrina, he also looked smug. Grazia could
tell, as soon as they had met, that neither of them believed
in the possibility of a "student killer."

Matera: "You know, Ispettore, I just can't imagine it
happening here—in Bologna, of all places! Do you
know what would happen? All hell would break loose!
I won't give it another thought." Sarrina had been both

more direct and adverse: "It sounds like a case for Ispetorre Callaghan, but this is not America."

To both of them Grazia had replied: "My name is Grazia Negro, not Callaghan. I'm from Nardo, a town in the province of Lecce."

"Done," the lab technician announced as he peeled the negatives away from his microsope. "We've got a beautiful negative — three fingers, ten out of ten papillary crests. Ispettore, I want you to know that these constitute the supermodels of fingerprints. In fifteen minutes, if he's got a police record, I'll be able to give you his name, address, and phone number."

"Be careful," Grazia said. "And don't forget to check the psychiatric hospitals and student records, too." The technician nodded, waved affirmatively, and moved off. Sarrina wouldn't stop staring at her; his amused gaze was now both ironic and brazen. It seemed to Grazia that he was staring directly at her breasts, which made her feel exposed. She was going to say something when Matera spoke up first.

"So, what's the plan? The questore told us you're in charge. That's fine with me. But what's the plan?"

Grazia's mouth felt dry. She felt uneasy in front of these two highly experienced and suspicious officers, just like the first time she had been alone with Vittorio in his office in Rome. She could tell Matera didn't like receiving orders from an equal-ranking female officer as young as herself. But what about Sarrina? You're too rough, too direct, a girlfriend had told her once. How will you ever manage to get a boyfriend when you're so straightforward?

"You got something to say, Sarrina?" There, she had spoken, rough and direct. Sarrina let his gaze rise slowly from her shoes to her face, until he was looking her straight in the eye. Then he smiled, lewdly.

"I know what you women in the police force are like, Ispettore. You always try so fucking hard to show that you're better than men . . ."

"Not true."

". . . it's always work, work, work. I bet you're some officer's daughter. I bet you don't have a boyfriend. I bet you won't even spread your legs until you're commissario capo."

"No way."

"So dress like a woman, for Christ's sake!"

Grazia folded her arms across her chest, fuck the pain, fuck her period, fuck everybody.

"My father had his own bar. He wanted me to become a bartender. I'm an officer because I like it, and I like to do it well. I'll probably never become commissario because I never got my university degree. Tell me, if I dressed like a woman, where the fuck would I carry my gun?"

To emphasize her point she turned around and lifted up her jacket to show the holster on her belt but when she realized that Sarrina had gotten up from his chair to admire her body, she turned around quickly, pissed off.

"Let's cut the crap. I took all the same criminal psychology courses that you both did, but I'm not interested in normal criminals. I'm only interested in serial killers. See, it's a territorial thing, Ispettore Matera — serial killers are often perpetual predators with a unique sense of space. Their victims have particular characteristics. Take Peter Sutcliffe, for example, the Yorkshire Ripper, who killed prostitutes around Leeds. Or Ed Kemper, who used to pick up hitchikers in the Berkeley area. Jeffrey Dahmer went to homosexual bars near Milwaukee. The Mostro di Firenze used to hang around Scandicci looking for couples. The man we're looking for is killing university students right here in Bologna. To find them, to win their confidence, and to gain entry into their homes, he's going to their clubs, their bars, their cafés. If we can pin a name and face on him, it shouldn't be too difficult to find him in a city the size of Bologna."

Total silence. No handshakes. No "Welcome aboard, Ispettore Negro." Nothing at all. Sarrina just kept staring at her in his lewd, laughing way. Matera raised his eyes to the ceiling with a paternalistic sigh.

"This city isn't like others, Ispettore Negro," he said. "You'll find that out soon enough. Let's just hope he has a criminal record."

"He does."

The lab technician came toward them, a file in his hands. They could see a photograph stapled to one of its corners and a thin line of writing next to it. Grazia stepped away from the filing cabinets and took it out of his hands. She put it down on the table. Matera and Sarrina stepped up behind her. Matera glanced at it and smiled; Sarrina laughed drily.

The photograph clipped to the file showed a boy who couldn't have been more than twenty. It showed him from the chest up, on a white background. His arms hung down by his sides. The sleeves of his gray T-shirt were rolled up to his shoulders. He had short, cropped, black hair, a lock of which lay flat across his forehead. His eyes were half-closed and he smiled lazily. There was a gap between his front teeth. Average height, average build, average weight. Next to the picture it read:

Alessio Crotti

Born: Cadoneghe (PD) October 26, 1972.

Committed to the Bologna Psychiatric Hospital on January 21, 1986.

Deceased: December 30, 1989.

—"Via Galliera, number 51 . . . the Rizzoli Hospital
. . . Viale Filopanti, at the corner of San Donato . . .
Strada Maggiore, number 38 . . . the back entrance of
the Hotel Pullman . . . Via Ferrarini . . . Via Ferrarini . . .
anybody on Via Ferrarini?"

—"This is Siena Termini 18, come in. Hi Anna, it's
me, Walter. You know, the one who takes the toughest
calls? I'll go to Via Ferrarini but tell the guy he'll have to
wait until I find out where it is. Hey, let's make a bet. If I
get there in five minutes you have dinner with me
tomorrow night. Hey Anna, did anyone ever tell you that
you have the sexiest voice of all the dispatch operators?"

Once, when I was young, I fell in love with a voice.
It happened a long time ago, when I used to go to the
school for blind kids, on the school bus, on the way
home. The bus driver always kept his radio on the same
station. One summer there was a radio show that would
begin shortly after we left the school; it always opened
with the same song. Every day, I'd try and be the first
one in line for the bus so that I could get the seat that
faced the speakers. Then, eight or ten minutes down the

road, the ads would end and the show would begin—
with that incredible song.

Now that I'm older, I know that the song was "La
Vie en Rose," but when I was younger all I knew was
that it was a beautiful song, that it was sung by a beautiful woman, and that she had a beautiful voice. It was a
sweet song, full of *R* sounds, but not the hard, green
ones. They were soft, pink *R*s. I never understood the
words and I never learned the singer's name. None of
that really mattered. In my mind she was The Pink R
Woman. I was in love with her as only a child can be.

—"This is Sovrintendente Avezzano to headquarters. Come in. Our shift is over. Ripamonti and I are
bringing the car back in. . . . Here, hang up the transmitter, would you? And make sure you turn it off. . . .
Hey, Teresina, what do you say? You want to go up
to San Luca and hang out for a while before we take
the car back? We've got more than half an hour and we
can always say that there was traffic on the highway. What do you mean? Are you telling me to fuck
off? Oh, I get it, it's your wedding band, is it? Well, I'm
married too—so what? We were both married last
time, remember?"

—"Come in Roma Termini 18 . . . Roma Termini
18? Walter, are you going to pick up that guy or not?
He called again and he's getting pissed off . . . if he com-
plains about me it'll be my third time this week and I'll
get fired for sure. Loris says that Via Ferrarini is near the
Pilastro, you know, where those three cops got killed

last week . . . step on it, Walter. . . . If you pick up this guy fast enough, I'll go out with you all week . . ."

My father was still alive that summer, and when I got home from school he would take me down to the court-yard of the building so that I could play with the other kids. We used to play a game called Blind Fly, which is sort of like hide and seek: the other kids would run away and I'd have to try to tag them as they ran by. Or we'd play Ghost Ball: I would stand in one of the garages and they'd kick the ball toward me and try to make a goal. I'd have to try and stop the ball just by listening to the sound of the ball or the movement of their feet. When the games with me were over or when they'd decide to go bike riding or play real soccer, then I'd go back to my house.

—"This is Rambo—Rambo here—come in, any-one? If anybody's out there, come in, because I've got to tell you about El Diablo . . . that maniac just passed me on the Via Emilia, just beyond Ferrara, without even waving. And you know where he's hurrying off to? With his extra load and everything? He's on his way to Casalecchio, to Luana! Maradona? Is that you, Mara-dona? El Diablo is in love!"

—"Wait a second, Terri, let me lower the seat. I want to look at you . . . god, you've got great tits . . . you like that, don't you? You like it like that, huh? . . . Feel it baby, feel how hard I am . . . it feels good, doesn't it? You want all of it, don't you Terri, . . . oh baby, that feels good. . . . It's so hard . . . feels good, doesn't it? . . ."

—"Anna? It's me, Walter. Look, Via Ferrarini is nowhere near the Pilastro. I think it's up in the hills somewhere. . . . Well, for chrissakes, you could have asked . . . for a cross street or something, anything. Wait, just take out the map and let me hear that sexy voice of yours tell me which direction because now I'm lost too . . ."

Sometimes, between games of Blind Fly and Ghost Ball, the kids would go sit on the courtyard wall. Sometimes I'd go with them. That particular summer they talked a lot about women they liked and I listened, even though I didn't understand everything they were talking about. They didn't mean the girls who lived in our building, they meant the ones on TV and in the movies and in magazines. Once they asked me who I liked, but what could I say? How could I explain to them that I liked The Pink R Woman because she had a blue voice? One day, when there was no school because of a strike, I brought my radio down to the courtyard and when the program came on I let all the guys hear The Pink R Woman singing "La Vie en Rose."

—"This is El Diablo—come in Rambo—come in Rambo. Listen, you prick! What the hell are you saying? I'm speeding because if I don't deliver my load before midnight they're gonna get my ass, not to mention Luana's!"
—"Holy shit, Terri! . . . you left the transmitter on. Everyone heard us! Mauro and everybody else

down at the goddamn station house! I told you to make sure it was turned off!"

—"Fuck you, Walter. The guy just called back and he took down my name . . ."

"This one?" they asked me. "But she's old-sounding! She's probably dead . . ."

—"Screw you, Anna, and your sexy voice!"

I ran upstairs, left the radio in the courtyard, and never went down there again. Later that summer my father died, and I stopped going to school. I never heard that radio show again. Never heard that song again. Or a blue voice—until the other night.

That's why I'm listening to the city tonight, with Chet Baker playing softly in the background.

Blue voice, where are you?

Blue voice, where are you?

Grazia lay down across the bed crosswise, shoving the pillows behind her back for support. She stuck out a leg, hooked a straight-backed chair with the tip of her boot, dragged it toward the bed, and rested both her feet on it. Her legs ached. The weight of her combat boots pulled at her ankles; she brought her knees in toward her chest one at a time, undid the buckles and laces, and kicked her boots off. The effort left her almost breathless. The toes of the white crew socks she wore under her boots were black, so she pulled her socks off. Grazia closed her eyes and rubbed her feet together, it sounded like a small sigh of relief. Slowly, she reached into the pocket of her bomber jacket, which she still had on, pulled out her cell phone, and dialed a number.

"Hi Vittorio, it's me," she started to say, but was interrupted by the answering machine: "Telecom Italia Mobile. Your call is being transferred to the voice mail box of . . . leave a message after the tone."

"Vittorio—it's me, Grazia. It's 10:30. I'm calling you from the room they've given me at the barracks. I have news for you: Another student's been killed. The killer bears a physical resemblance to Maurizio Assirelli, the boy that was killed in the previous homicide, but his fingerprints correspond to someone named Alessio Crotti, who died in a psychiatric hospital in December 1989. This persona, made up of two dead individuals, decided not to leave the victim's apartment right away. He stayed there for a couple of days, used the computer, went on-line and into chat rooms. The name of the most recent victim is Paolo Miserocchi: his nickname was Misero. He was a student and drug dealer. I don't believe in ghosts, Vittorio, but it's starting to look like you've sent me on a hunt for a zombie in a city I barely know. Sorry, I give up. Tomorrow I'm taking the train back to Rome. If you want to talk, you can call me. My number is 0338-245863. Ciao."

Grazia flipped the cell phone shut and let it drop next to her on the bed. She took the figurine out of her pocket and held it up to the light. With the other hand she massaged her swollen belly. Suddenly, she stood up, took off her coat, took her dress off over her head, and let it fall to the floor. She stuck her thumbs into the top of her tights and peeled them off, hopping first on one leg and then the other. She started to take off her camisole but then shivered and kept it on. She walked over to the desk, rummaged around in a drawer, found a pencil, pulled her hair up into a bun, and stuck the pencil through it. She picked up her laptop and a thick green file of papers and sat down on the side of the bed.

With her foot, she cleared away some space on the floor where she had dropped her jacket. She took the photograph of Alessio Crotti, who died on December

30, 1989, from the file and placed it there. She put the glass lizard on top of his face. Because of the cyano-acrylate that still clouded the figurine, the face in the photograph under it appeared distorted.

"You know what I like about you, Ispettore Negro," Vittorio had told her a long time ago, when he began to address her as a colleague. "I like your fierce, animal instinct. You have a keen sense of judgment. That's why I had you assigned to UASC. We have psychiatrists, criminologists, analysts, and theoreticians . . . we needed you, sweetheart." When he called her sweetheart, she felt a strange tingling run through her that made her blush. A keen sense of judgment. Fierce, animal instincts. Fierce, keen.

Grazia let the picture of the Assirelli boy fall to the floor. It landed on top of her dress, next to the photo of Alessio Crotti. Maurizio Assirelli had a round face, dark skin, shaped sideburns, and a goatee, just like Anna Bulzamini Lazzaroni (like the *biscotti* company) had described. He wore headphones. She thought about that—headphones. She sat very still.

Grazia jumped up, went to the desk and grabbed her modem wire, her bare feet smacking the cold, hard tiles. She plugged one end of the wire into her computer and connected the other to her cell phone. She clicked twice on an icon. She heard the modem dialing up the server at the Rome Questura. Grazia entered her SCIPS password and clicked on the directory *SK-Bologna*, then opened the file where all the witness reports were stored.

She sat crosslegged in front of her computer, peering closely at the screen. She had completely forgotten about her cramps.

There had been no witness reports for the first victim, the student from Palermo who was killed in his apartment in the Hills. Nor had there been any for the second victim, the junkie from San Lazzaro. But in the report on the couple that had been murdered in Castenaso, somebody had seen a strange young man wearing headphones—a very skinny boy who looked like a junkie and had short dreadlocks.

Grazia reached into the green file and took out a photograph. Marco Lucchesi, age twenty-seven, born in Genova, etc., etc. Previously arrested for possession and trafficking, etc., etc. Died in San Lazzaro on November 15, 1995. The photo in the file was of a very skinny boy who looked like a junkie and had short dreadlocks.

Grazia stood up. She fiddled with her bra straps, paced up and down the room, then sat back down in front of the computer. The Lucchesi case. Among the witness reports there was one filed by the hunter who found the naked body in a ditch at four in the morning, one by the local police who responded to the call, and one by the highway patrol, when they found an abandoned red Citroën Due Cavalli two days later, near Ferrara. A red Citroën Due Cavalli.

Grazia went back to the Graziano case. Upper-middle-class family. Rental apartment in the hills above Bologna. Closet homosexual. When the victim disappeared, his family went on *Chi l'ha visto?*, the weekly TV program for unsolved cases to enroll the public's help. In the following episode, they received word that the boy had been seen, but in the meantime, the police had found his naked body, so the tip was ignored. This information wasn't among the computer files but Grazia had watched the episode. She had studied it closely, just like everything else having to do with the case. The caller had said that an effeminate looking young man with a closely trimmed small beard, leather jacket, and headphones had been seen getting into a red Due Cavalli near San Lazzaro. Headphones. Closely trimmed beard and leather jacket. Effeminate. Grazia let the picture of Marco Graziano, age twenty-five, fall to the floor. It was his university ID photograph. He wore a closely trimmed goatee beard and leather jacket and looked slightly effeminate.

"Shit," Grazia thought to herself. Her gaze shifted from her computer to the photograph of Alessio Crotti. From where she was, through the distorting light of the glass lizard, it looked like his mouth was open in a desperate, mute howl.

In each case the victim of the prior homicide was somehow present.

Grazia unplugged her computer. She practically tore the modem wire out of her cell phone. She let her hair down, then pulled it back up again, in an even tighter bun, so tight it hurt. She ran into the bathroom and splashed cold water on her face. She wet her mouth with her hand. She needed to talk to Vittorio.

When she got back to the bed, she realized that she

had left the cell phone turned off; there was already one message.

"Hello? Grazia? where the hell are you? It's always busy. Listen: what was that delirious message about? Is it your period? Who is this Alessio Crotti guy? I'll run a check, but you look into the chat room . . . get the hard drive analyzed and try and figure out who was calling who. As for the rest, including that bullshit about coming back to Rome, I'll just ignore it. Ciao, sweetheart."

Grazia dialed Vittorio's number, her fingers flying over the numbers. While listening to it ring, she gently rubbed her smooth backside. Then, absentmindedly, she sat down on the side of the bed and started wiping a toenail with her index finger. "Telecom Italia Mobile. Your call has been . . . leave a message after the tone."

"Shit. Where the hell are *you*, Vittorio? Your answering machine is always on. Listen. This is not a delirium, it's an investigative hypothesis. If you run a check on the links between the cases you'll notice something strange. The homosexual boy gets killed and they find his body in the country, but a few days later he's seen wearing a pair of headphones in the junkie's neighborhood when *he* gets killed. Then the junkie reappears, also wearing headphones, this time around Castenaso, when the couple gets killed. Today someone that resembles Maurizio Assirelli, who's already dead, is seen (with headphones) in the apartment of the boy whose body we just found! I haven't checked on it yet, but I'll bet you that somewhere in the Assirelli case there's an Andrea Farolfi lookalike, who was killed six months earlier. I'd bet my balls (which I don't have) that somewhere in Bologna, at this very moment, there's a guy walking around that looks a lot like Paolo Miserocchi, and he's probably wearing the same damn headphones."

Grazia's throat was dry. She had spoken quickly. "Do you see what I'm saying, Vittorio? Don't you get it? In each crime the victim of the previous crime reappears, reincarnated, ready to kill. You know what I think, Vittorio?"

Beep. "Your message will be forwarded . . ."

0338446022.

"Telecom Italia Mobile."

Grazia let go of her toe.

"You know what I think, Vittorio? Seeing that I don't believe in zombies or vampires or wolfmen, and seeing how the Assirelli kid and the all others have died, I think there has got to be a rational answer to all of this—and it all converges on Alessio Crotti. As for my period, Vittorio, don't you worry about that. I get it every month. And you know what? It helps me think."

She flipped shut the telphone, then reopened it to make sure that it was still turned on, before dropping it onto the pillow. The photograph of Alessio Crotti seemed to be howling at her. It almost scared her. She pushed the lizard off the picture with her foot, then covered his face with her big toe. She tapped her foot up and down over his face, feeling the patina of the paper stick to her toe, watching his face disappear and then reappear, looking desperate and frightening. Suddenly, Grazia felt a slow release in her belly and dampness between her legs. Finally. She grabbed her bomber jacket by the collar and ran into the bathroom, took the tampons out of her pocket and slipped out of her pants. She scratched at the tongue of cellophane and began to unwrap one when she heard the phone ring. For a second she didn't move, but then she dropped the tampon into the sink, wedged a towel between her legs, and ran to get the phone.

"Vittorio? Where the hell have you . . . ?"

But it wasn't Vittorio. It was a stranger's voice. A soft, nervous voice.

"What? What? Who is this? I can't hear you . . . how did you get my number?"

The voice at the other end faltered. He spoke and then hesitated in embarrassment. He heaped his words one on top of another. Something about a scanner. Headphones. Voices of the city. A green voice, her voice. He was chatting with a girl on-line, he asked her for her address.

"I don't understand. How did you get this information? You know that's illegal, don't you? What do you mean, a green voice? Did you see anything? Did you . . . What?? You're blind? You mean you can't see?"

Silence. Grazia looked up at the ceiling and sighed impatiently.

"Listen, give me your number and I'll call you back tomorrow and we can talk about it calmly. Hello? hello? Oh, fuck you."

Grazia snapped the phone shut. When it rang again, she almost dropped it. She got to her feet; the towel fell to the ground.

"Listen, what the hell . . . ?"

"Grazia, is that you? It's me, Vittorio."

Vittorio. Grazia breathed a sigh of relief and instinctively pulled her camisole down to cover herself up.

"What's the matter? Who did you think it was?"

"No one, it's just that we've only begun working on this case and the crank calls are already coming in. Someone must have intercepted my calls."

"OK. You'll tell me about it later. I thought about your message and did a little research . . . it seems that Alessio Crotti died in a psychiatric hospital, but it's all very hazy. A portable heater in the 4th Ward of the hospital had a short-circuit and there was a fire. The flames hit the oxygen tanks and there was a huge explosion. The doctor on duty and three inmates were blown sky-high over Bologna."

"So he's alive. His fingerprints are all over Paolo Miserocchi's things. He walked through fire. Like an iguana."

"Salamanders do that, sweetheart. But you're right. Anyway, I like iguanas better. Besides, if your hypothesis holds up, this Alessio Crotti, or whoever he is, changes skin each time . . . just like iguanas do. Let's try and figure out how and why. Well done for now, sweetheart. Good work."

Grazia smiled. She picked the towel up from the floor and put it on the bed, then sat down next to it. She pulled her knees into her chest, one foot crossed over the other, chin resting on her knees.

"Wait, Vittorio, before you go: the police have the student's hard drive and won't hand it over. The way things are going we won't get our hands on it for another month, if that."

"I suppose our friend Dottor Alvau still hasn't decided if he wants to win a glorious case or just avoid a pain in the ass. I'll talk to him. I'll let him know how favorable the press on this could be. Are you all right?"

"Yes."

"Are you tired?"

"No."

"Good, because you know what you have to do, don't you? Go down to headquarters, send out an APB, file a wanted card, and get a poster made for a Paolo Miserocchi lookalike. We've got to do it fast before the Iguana kills again. If he changes his identity, the wanted posters won't mean a thing. It's like being blind."

Grazia's heels thudded to the floor in surprise.

"What did you just say?"

"Did I say something? What did I just say?"

"Never mind, it doesn't matter. Tomorrow. I've got to get dressed now and go down to the Questura."

"Why, you're naked?"

"Ciao, Vittorio."

"Ciao, sweetheart. Good work. Really. I mean it."

Grazia got up and walked slowly toward the bathroom. The voice of the anonymous caller came back to her.

"No, impossible," she thought to herself.

Like being blind, he had said. No way.

Good work, sweetheart, he had said. *Good work.*

If he changes identity again, his face won't matter. Impossible.

She felt damp and sticky. She had to wash up, get dressed and run down to headquarters. Wanted posters. APB. Paolo Miserocchi. Iguanas change skin.

We'd be better off with someone who could recognize his voice. No way—impossible.

When she finished showering, she hurried over to her suitcase, which she had left open on the table, kicking the glass figurine by mistake and sending it flying across the room. It hit the wall and cracked in two.

A blind man. Impossible.

Hey, Rita . . . you think we could get together sometime?
Why don't we get together now?

"Usually I don't let anyone come up," she says.

"But I feel different about you. Right away I knew you were different. I could feel it," she says.

"If my father knew you were up here, he'd kill me," she says.

She's sitting on a chair, leaning on a small foldaway kitchen table with her elbow. The room is a tiny studio apartment, squeezed in under a beamed roof. Everything is a different color: the walls, fixtures, chairs, rugs, posters, Buddha statues, and stuffed animals. It looks like a kaleidoscope. I'm sitting on the sofa, just a few feet away from her.

"I understand you; I know the way you are," she says.

"I feel like I've known you forever," she says.

"You're kind—sensitive and kind," she says.

She's sitting on a chair, leaning on the kitchen table, pulling at the collar of her orange T-shirt. She's fiddling with a leather cord that she's wearing around her neck. Occasionally a small copper Aquarius pendant appears.

She's sitting with one leg crossed at a right angle over the other, baggy Indian pants gathered at the calf. She's wearing an anklet made of red, yellow, and green cotton strands. I'm sitting on the sofa, just a few feet away.

"Hey, if the doorbell rings, don't worry, it's just a friend of mine from art school, he's covered with piercings, I mean totally covered, he's bringing me a cell phone," she says.

"Hey, it's not like I own one or anything. A friend of mine clones numbers and we rack up these wild bills," she says.

"Hey, this friend isn't my boyfriend or anything, I'm independent, you know what I mean? Especially on the inside, you know? I guess that's why I never seem to find the right guy," she says.

She's sitting on a chair and leaning on the table. She has a series of thin red scratches that extend in dash marks around her anklebone. Behind the bone, between two veins that stick out ever so slightly, there's a reddish mark, as if from an elastic band. The nail of her big toe is lustrous. There's a shiny, dark groove that runs down it. Me. A few feet away. From her. Sitting.

"Can you hear me with your earphones on?" she says.

"What are you mumbling? I can't hear you," she says.

"Why are you looking at me like that?" she says.

Then, without warning, the skin on my face cracks into millions of fragments. It scales off the bones of my face, leaving my skull completely exposed. My eyeballs, no longer protected by the flap of eyelids, roll forward, frozen partway through their orbit. She's still staring at me. Doesn't she see what's happening? Me. A few feet away.

"Why are you looking at me like that?" she says.

Something, from somewhere inside my head, pushes the bones of my face forward. My eyes swell up and push against the arc of my lashes—I know they're going to explode. How can she not see what's happening?

"Why are you looking at me like that?" she says.
"Why are you looking at me like that?"
"OH MY GOD, WHY ARE YOU LOOKING AT ME LIKE THAT?"

WHY ARE YOU LOOKING AT ME LIKE THAT?

Part II

Reptile

Angel bleed from the tainted touch of my caress
need to contaminate to alleviate this loneliness . . .
        —Nine Inch Nails, "Reptile"

There's a handwritten note in pencil from Vittorio attached to the first page. He writes fast, his scrawled letters push at the limits of comprehension:

"The life, death, and miracles of Alessio Crotti, aka The Iguana. We'll talk when I get back from Washington. Good work, sweetheart."

The letterhead on the first page reads:
UNIT FOR THE ANALYSIS OF SERIAL CRIMES (UASC)
Then:
PSYCHOLOGICAL OFFENDER PROFILE (POP)

A BEHAVIORAL PROFILE OF ALESSIO CROTTI, BORN IN CADONEGHE (PD) OCTOBER 26, 1972 AND SUSPECTED OF THE FOLLOWING FELONIES.

Farther down on the bright, white inkjet printer paper there's the blue rubber stamp of the police messenger service. And the date: MARCH 21, 1997.

The heading on the second page says:
EXCERPTS FROM THE DEPOSITION MADE BY DOTT. FRANCESCO MARIANI, JUVENILE NEUROPSYCHIATRIST.

The report is typewritten, all the G's are lopsided, the ink is slightly faded, the paper is yellowed and dry. Vittorio had underlined certain passages in pencil.

. . . Purely for the sake of clarity and not to blame others, I would like to make it known that I met with Alessio Crotti on one occasion alone. At that time (July 12, 1983) he was 11 years old and a boarder at the Pious Institute for Children. During our meeting I verified the following:

• that the masturbatory activity of Alessio Crotti, which, according to the administrators of the Pious Institute, was the central motive for our meeting, was completely normal for his age and pubescent phase;

• that the *auditory troubles* that Alessio Crotti had complained of (partial deafness, the *perception of indefinite sounds, whistling*) were medically unfounded and could be seen as efforts to draw attention to himself, which, for a child who has been institutionalized since the age of five, can be considered completely normal;

• the same can be said for his habits of *chewing the skin off his finger tips* and *looking at himself in the mirror* for extended periods of time.

Despite the child's tendency to isolate himself and his somewhat taciturn character, he seemed intelligent enough and capable of sound judgment. As such, I assessed him as healthy and perfectly normal.

Nobody ever mentioned the *Games Room incident* to me or that he suffered from recurring nightmares or that he entertained *dragon fantasies*. The teachers and proctors alike had only spoken to me of his frequent masturbatory activity.

In the margin Vittorio had written, "What dragons? What Games Room incident?" An arrow at the bottom right corner of the page indicated to go to the next page.

The third page was made of thick, gray, recycled paper. The commas were dark and heavy and slightly in relief from the rest of the text. In the margin, in gold lettering, it read:

OMG—SÃO-BERNARDO PROJECT—SAVE THE FORESTS.

Deposition of Father Girolamo Montuschi, Pious Institute for Children.

I would like to begin by stating that I am neither a psychiatrist nor a psychologist, but only a simple man of the cloth, a friar. It is not my duty to pass judgment. When one thinks about young Alessio Crotti, one must immediately take into consideration that he was conceived out of wedlock, that his natural father refused to acknowledge his existence and that his mother had to enroll him in the Insitute because *the man she lived with did not want the child in their home.* Alessio's mother, Albertina Crotti, died when Alessio was twelve. In the many years he was with us, she only came to visit him about ten times, at the most. He was practically an orphan.

This is why I was not overly concerned when, at the age of five or six, Alessio began to wake up in the middle of the night because of recurring nightmares. He screamed so loudly that he would wake up all the children in his dormitory room. He said that he dreamt about a scabrous dragon that would, as he put it, "jump onto his chest and eat his face off." As we had recently watched a documentary on television entitled *Galapagos: The Last Dragons,* and as it had had an effect on many other children besides Alessio, I was not excessively concerned about his nightmares. Alessio, in fact, had often expressed a keen interest in exotic animals and distant tribes and other such adventurous things.

My worries intensified some time later. I recall one night in particular when Father Filippo woke me up to inform me that young Alessio was not in his bed and that no one knew where he was. We looked for him everywhere, finding him finally in the Games Room, on the other side of the Refectory, at the far end of the Institute. It was dark. He was standing completely naked in front of a mirror, painting circles on his face with colored pens.

We punished him in our usual manner; as the event never repeated itself, I eventually forgot about the whole episode.

A blue Post-it note was stuck on the left-hand side of the page, about halfway down.

It was from Vittorio.

"You see what happens, sweetheart? He takes off his clothes and looks at himself in the mirror. He paints his face like the Maori warriors he's seen in books. He dreams about the iguanas on the Galapagos Islands. He covers his face with a mask: why?

He hears noises: what kind?

Get him, sweetheart.

And find the blind guy."

Last night I dreamed about her.

I have my own way of dreaming. Waves of solid heat glide over my body, across my face, and over my fingertips. I dream of smells wrapping around me, enveloping me. I dream of tastes that I can move through, that I can touch and squeeze. But above all, I dream of sounds. Last night I heard the sound of her blue voice melting inside my head, the way snow melts in the palm of your hand. But it wasn't cold, it was warm. And sweet. And through my nose, I smelled steel and smoke—strong and cool, the way the morning smells through a wide, open window.

The dream lasted a long time. I felt its soft weight somewhere between my heart and my stomach even after I woke up, and for much of the morning.

But I didn't call in.

I heard her voice several times on the radio. There was even something on the television news and in the papers. My mother came upstairs to ask if I was the witness they were looking for. All they were saying was that a blind person had contacted them a week ago with valuable information and that he should call Ispettore Negro as soon as possible. Urgently. Please.

I didn't do it.

In all the years that I've been listening to the voices of the city on my scanner, I've heard lots of addresses, names, and phone numbers. But I have never gotten involved, never contacted anyone. Why should I? What could I say? What could I ever hope to hear? It was different the night I called her. She breathed her words with such intensity and enthusiasm, yet they trembled on her lips, as if she were scared to utter them. I wanted to help her. I wanted to help her speak the words, to ease them through her mouth, to help her blow a beautiful, full note—a strong solo. I wanted to put a little red and yellow into her blue voice. I wanted to help her.

I didn't call in, though. I knew she'd find me.

My mother.

"Simone, are you up there? There are some people here that want to talk to you."

I get up and touch the lightbulb on the desk lamp to make sure it's off. Then I go over to the sofa and lie down, pull my legs up to my chest, and turn toward the wall. But it doesn't work.

"Simone? Oh my, it's so dark in here . . . sorry, let me get the light for you. Sometimes he keeps it on for days and days and other times, well, you know. Simone, what are you doing? Are you asleep?"

The flip of the switch tells me they've turned on the light in my room. And that there are people. Lots of them. My mother moves gently through the room, turning the swivel chair at my desk around and saying, "Please, make yourself comfortable" and then, "Simone, come on now, sit up." A man at the door breathes heavily, through his teeth, as if he's a smoker. Another man is standing next to him, looking around and jangling small change in his pocket, making the flat, dead sound that coins make.

But where is she?

"Signor Martini, I'm Ispettore Negro. With me here are Ispettore Matera and Ispettore Sarrina, both from the Polizia di Stato. I'm glad you decided to see . . . I mean, meet us."

I don't say anything. I sit up and fold my arms across my chest. I hear rubber soles coming toward me. I listen to the way her mouth opens, the way she takes a quick breath before speaking, as if she wants to inflate the words so they come out of her mouth faster and closer together. I can tell she's embarrassed.

"My name is Grazia, I'm twenty-six, I'm about medium height and dark-haired. I'm wearing an olive-green bomber jacket, and I'm standing in front of you, Mr. Martini."

"So?"

"Simone!" my mother exclaims.

"I thought you might want to know what I look like. I noticed you were looking the other way . . ."

"I'm not looking anywhere, Ispettore. I can't 'look.'"

"Simone!"

"I'm sorry. I meant I thought that you might want to visualize me."

I smile.

"Oh really? How would I do that?"

"Simone!"

She doesn't say a word. I hear the scratch of a synthetic fiber, as if she has turned away. For a moment I think she might be leaving. No, I don't *think*. I fear she's leaving. But I don't hear the soles of her shoes. It's just that her voice has shifted direction.

"I'd like a few moments alone with Signor Martini, please. If you don't mind, Signora."

The Breather takes a heavy breath.

"It'll only be a few minutes, Signora," Small Change says to my mother.

"Well . . ." my mother says. I hear the door handle clear its throat and the door closes with a sigh. "Well, I don't know . . ." my mother's saying, farther away, from the staircase. "Well . . ."

We're alone. The wheels on the swivel chair roll toward me. The cushion on the seat whispers as she sits down. She must have her elbows on her knees because I can feel her voice close to my face.

"Signor Martini—may I call you Simone?—can we talk?"

"No."

"Listen, Simone . . ."

Why do I hear the sound of faraway music all of a sudden? It's almost like a fold in a cloth that disappears as soon as I reach out to touch it. It's the beginning of something, the opening of a piece of music that I can't quite remember.

"I owe you an apology. I should have listened to you when you called me the first time. If I had, we might have saved the girl. But I was distracted, I had other things on my mind, and honestly, I didn't understand much of what you were saying."

I notice a quick movement, like two notes being played together. It dissolves so quickly I barely notice it. What is it? It has to do with her smell. I heard the music at the same time that I noticed her smell. She doesn't have a very pretty smell. It's a combination of stale smoke, the cold fabric of her coat, sweat, and something sweet, like blood, the way my mother sometimes smells. The music, though, has nothing to do with any of those. It's completely different.

"Anyway, it's my fault. I'll have to live with it for the rest of my life. But I can't think about that now. There's no time. I have to catch this person. I wish you could see the photograph of the girl, the way we found her. Stupidly, I brought it with me without thinking that a nonseeing person —"

"I'm not a nonseeing person. I'm blind."

She sighs. I feel her breath on my face and immediately I hear that distant, fleeting music. It sounds just like her breath feels, first there's a coolness on my cheeks and mouth and then, warmth.

"Listen, Simone, quit correcting me. I know each time I say something I make a mistake. If you want, I can learn. Maybe you can teach me, but afterward. Not now. There's no time. There's a maniac going around Bologna killing people in the most horrible way. We call him the Iguana because it's as if he changes skin after each murder; he always looks different. He takes on a new identity. This time, though, we have no new image to go by because the girl he killed was found with her clothes on. He must have left the apartment with someone else. I'd be happy to give you all the details but there's not much time now, Simone."

That music. It opens with a bass and then there's a guitar, and then? Grass. Green, green grass. Freshly cut grass.

"You're the only person who knows how to recognize the Iguana. You're the only one who has heard him speak. You told me you heard his voice. Your mother told us that you listen to the scanner all day, so Vittorio and I thought that you . . ."

"Who's Vittorio?"

"He's my boss. Vittorio Poletto. He's one of the superivisors of UASC. I'll tell you about that later, too. In the girl's apartment we found a spare battery for a cell phone so we think he might use a cell phone soon, or go on-line. We think, or rather, we hope his message can be intercepted by a scanner like yours. We'd like you to stay tuned to the scanner to see if you hear him. You're the only one who can recognize him. Simone, we want you to help us. But we don't have a lot of time, so just say yes or no. Right away. Yes or no. Now."

She moves closer to me on the swivel chair. Its wheels creak rustily. All of a sudden I smell her so clearly and vividly that I remember the music. It's "Summertime." Not the majestic, vaguely sad version that you usually hear, but the old, crackly one that gets used in the deodorant advertisment. That's the smell. It's overpowered by the smoke on her jacket and by the acidulous sweetness of her skin, but I smell the cool smell of deodorant when she gets close to me. It might not actually be the same deodorant as in the ad. That doesn't matter. Just like it doesn't really matter what musical, linguistic, or mnemonic associations I made in order to figure it out. All I know is that from now on she will be that music for me. Every time I think of her or hear her speak, I'll think of that music. And I know that if I couldn't hear it any more, I'd miss her.

That's why—even if I'm scared, even if I don't really want to help—I bite my lip and say, "Yes. All right. I'll help."

The single ring on her cell phone informed Grazia that she had e-mail. There was a message in Eudora, *from* v. poletto@mbox.vol.it *to* gnegro@mbox.queen.it, subject: Iguana. Three attached files.

She pointed the cursor to OK. Click.

I'll call as soon as I get back from Milan.
Get him.
V.

File #1.
EXCERPT FROM THE DEPOSITION OF DOTT. DON GIUSEPPE CARRARO, PSYCHOLOGIST

Without wanting to aggravate the recent dispute and add to the finger-pointing, I would like to state my position and disprove the harsh accusations of having underestimated the gravity of Alessio Crotti's case.

Alessio was fourteen years old when we met. He had recently completed middle school at the Pious Institute and had won a scholarship to continue his studies in accounting at a vocational high school. He resided in a student housing unit with two boys who also had religious scholarships to support themselves while in school.

The relationship between the boys was fraught with tension from the outset. I was asked to intervene, both as psychologist and as religious counselor to the dormitory. The two boys complained that Alessio mumbled to himself constantly and that his music was excessively loud, even though he wore headphones.

I spoke with Alessio. He explained that he liked to say his prayers out loud; I suggested he pray in silence. That took care of one problem. As for the music, I prohibited it altogether. I am aware of the negative influence that certain music can have on young children and their delicate souls. (Numerous studies show just how evil this so-called "satanic rock" really is !!)

For about a year things went smoothly. Alessio behaved well, applied himself to his studies, participated in Sunday Mass and received Communion on a regular basis.

I had no idea that it would ever come to this. How, in God's name, could I ever have imagined such a thing?

File #2

POLICE HEADQUARTERS OF BOLOGNA. TERRITORIAL COMMAND CENTER. REPORT # 1234.

I, Nicola Alfano, commander of Patrol Car 3, together with agent Michele De Zan, report that on March 19, 1986, at 2100h we received an emergency call from headquarters instructing us to go to the second floor of the Student Housing Unit at 35 Via Boccain-dosso. Once at the location, we detected screaming coming from Apartment 17. We broke in with force. A young male was on the floor. We administered emergency medical attention. After verifying his demise, I proceeded down the hallway. Agent De Zan, shocked by the condition of the victim, remained in the main vestibule. A second young male was hiding under a table at the end of the hallway. I extracted my regulation handgun and proceeded toward the kitchen area. There, I encountered a third young male, subsequently identified as Alessio Crotti, age 15. The boy was naked, in front of the open refrigerator, screaming and spreading mustard over his face. He had worked himself into such a frenzy that it was difficult for me to immobilize and handcuff him.

File #3

He needs a mask behind which he can hide. He takes off his clothes and paints his face like a primitive man because he doesn't understand that he already has a face. And all because of that horrible March night. The violence he displayed toward his roommates is just the beginning; the hospital does the rest.

You know what happens, sweetheart?

The Iguana gets committed to the Psychiatric Ward of the prison hospital. He's given the standard treatment: every fifteen days he gets a 50mm. dose of Aloperidolo Decanoato. They take his fingerprints, the ones you found on the statuette. They run tests on him. They do hypnotic and cognitive therapy. He stays there for three years. Then—boom!—Pavilion 4 explodes and Alessio Crotti escapes, freed of that identity.

But he feels naked now.

He needs a new identity.

A mask.

That's how we have the Iguana.

That's why he kills people. Butchers them. Mutilates them. He nullifies them. Tears off their clothes. He tears off his own clothes and puts on theirs, as if he were putting on a second skin.

But why? What is he running away from? What does he think about when he's alone? When he lies down, curled up like a fetus, immersed in his music as if it's some kind of amniotic liquid? What is he afraid of?

Get him, sweetheart.

Get him, sweetheart.

Piazza Verdi, a rectangular shaped piazza in the center of Bologna, is traversed by Via Zamboni, the road that leads to the university. If you're traveling up Via Zamboni with the flow of traffic, about halfway up its length it gently curves to the left. The porticoes on either side of the road follow the curve. There, quite suddenly, it opens onto the piazza. Five other roads, each with its own passageway of porticoes, extend off the piazza like rays of a sun in a child's drawing. It's damp and shady under the porticoes, even on an April afternoon. The warmth of spring doesn't reach under them. And when it's cloudy outside, the porticoes are bereft of light.

Get him.

Grazia had never liked the porticoes. Instead, she wandered slowly through the half-price bookstalls that had been set up in a corner of the piazza, between the cafeteria building and the now shuttered university cooperative store. The afternoon sun reflected off the white awnings of the bookstalls, as if they were tents in the Sahara. Grazia felt warm. She took off her bomber jacket and tied it loosely around her hips to hide her gun from view.

Get him, sweetheart.

She smiled wryly to herself and bit her lower lip in impatience. She tossed the book she had been pretending to look at back onto the cart; the vendor looked over to see what title could have provoked such a reaction.

Earlier, driving through the city in search of the murdered girl's roommate, Matera had told her that Bologna wasn't like other cities. It isn't what it seems, he said, tapping at the windshield with his knuckles and indicating "out there" with a toss of his head. You think it's small, he said to her, because you're looking at what lies within the city walls, which isn't much bigger than a big town. But that's not the way it really is, Ispettore. Not at all. The city called Bologna actually extends all the way from Parma, in the north, to Cattolica, on the Adriatic coast. The city grew up out of the old Via Emilia. There are people here who live in Modena, work in Bologna, and go dancing at night in Rimini. It's an odd metropolis—two million inhabitants in two thousand square kilometers. It spreads like an oil spill between the sea and the Appenine Mountains. And it has no real center, only marginal cities: Ferrara, Imola, Ravenna, the Adriatic coastal towns.

They found the roommate of the murdered girl in one of the squatter-occupied buildings on Via del Lazzaretto. Sara was twenty three, her hair was short and pink, one ear was pierced with multiple tiny earrings. She kept her hands inside the roomy sleeves of her oversize plaid shirt. She was edgy and kept pacing up and down the apartment, which, in most respects, resembled any other public housing unit. No: she moved out of Rita's place a long time ago. Money: for as long as she had been studying literature her father had been sending money orders from Naples, but when she quit, he stopped sending them. Four months ago: Ciao, Rita, I'm going to live rent-free with some squatters on Via Pratello. Then the city had made them clear out and they moved to this place on Via del Lazzaretto. Before moving out, however, Sara had found Rita a new roommate.

The light changes quickly in April. When the sun starts to go down, the shadows under the porticoes turn reddish, then, streaked by the few orange rays of sun that make their way through, they slide down the walls. It hurts your eyes to stare at the puddles of burning, reddish light that form at the base of the columns. When the sun goes behind the rooftops and the light becomes more opaque, darkened by the violet filter of the lowering clouds, then the shadows under the porticoes turn light gray. Then the color of steel. Then a deep, rich, ferrous, chrome-tinted color—almost blue. The entire piazza goes through a complete transformation. At a quarter past seven it's an entirely different place than it was fifteen minutes earlier.

Grazia noticed this as she was walking by the university library, where she stopped to bend down and tie her shoe. The custodian was at the door, locking up for the night. When Grazia straightened up, the custodian of the library was glaring at her but Grazia didn't take any notice. What struck Grazia, instead, were the brightly colored concert posters pasted on the passage-way walls, the graffiti scrawled on the columns, the spray-painted words in Arabic, the piles of flyers that had collected in the dark corners. The students had all disappeared. Even the junkie that usually stood in front of the Teatro Comunale begging for change had gone to sit down on the steps, his hands in his pockets.

This city isn't like others, Matera had said. It's not only big, it's complicated. It's contradictory. If you look at it from a pedestrian perspective, it seems like there are a lot of piazzas and porticoes. But if you fly over it in a helicopter, because of the courtyards and gardens between the buildings, it looks like there's a forest below. And if you go beneath its surface you'll find that it's a city built on water and canals, like Venezia. It's freezing cold in the winter and tropical in the summer. It has Communist ideals and millionaire cooperative organizations. It's run by four different mafia groups that, rather than shoot at each other, help each other recycle Italy's drug money. Tortellini and satanic cults. This city isn't what it seems, Ispettore; it's always hiding something.

Stefania, the last roommate of the murdered girl, was twenty-five years old, had straight, blond hair, was wearing a blue cardigan and a white blouse, a pearl brooch and a thin gold band on her finger. Business school. No really, after a couple of days I knew it wouldn't work out. She was, like, hysterical each time my cell phone rang. I was, like, go Buddha, go New Age music, it's relaxing, that's fine. But the incense made me sick. She would be, like, on-line all the time looking for her soul mate. She was the kind of person that would be part of a group suicide if some comet was passing by. I was, like, in a week I'm going on a study abroad program in London to get my master's degree in marketing. Stefania had already settled into a new apartment. She had seen an ad on the bulletin board in her department for a "renovated loft, no live-in (but no one checks) with two bedrooms, one bathroom, kitchen, three million lira to be split four ways." All four of the roommates were girls, from Pesaro and in the business school. The only problem in their living arrangement was figuring out whose cell phone was ringing.

Get him.

Grazia sat down at the base of a column under the porticoes at a point where the street was significantly lower than the sidewalk. She could barely touch the asphalt with her sneakers. She leaned forward and hugged her knees but then remembered her gun and straightened up, so it wouldn't poke out. She turned to see whether the junkie on the steps of the theater had noticed but he was absorbed with untying his sleeping bag.

Get him, sweetheart.

Shit.

This city isn't like others, Matera had said. You say you want to search the university — OK — we'll search the university, we'll sift through the students, we'll check out their clubs, apartments, cafeterias . . . but you know what, Ispettore Negro? The university isn't what it seems, either. The university has another side to it, and not much is known about it, either. Students come to Bologna from all parts of Italy. They start studying and then quit, then they start up again. They stay at friends' or relatives' houses, they sublet apartments illegally, with no guarantees or contracts. Did you know that most of the terrorists in the seventies lived in Bologna? Anywhere else in Italy someone would have noticed a weird looking kid with a strange accent, coming and going at all hours of the day and night, with no apparent job, disappearing for long stretches of time. But not here. Here, that's your basic student. You want to get to know the University, Ispettore? The University is its own clandestine city.

When they had been leaving, Stefania had added: "I remember she had a friend, he was covered with piercings, it was so gross. Once I even accompanied him home: 4 Via Altaseta, top floor." They found Nicola: twenty-seven years old, short and chubby, volume II of *Anatomy* open on the kitchen table in front of him. No piercings. Nope, I don't know anything about it, I'm just passing through. A friend of mine lent me his apartment so that I could study for my exams. If I don't pass I have to leave for military service and then I wouldn't need an apartment in Bologna. My friend? Well, actually he isn't really my friend, he's a friend of a friend. I only met him once, when he gave me the keys. Yeah, he was tall and covered with earrings. Yeah, my friend told me about him. They call him Luther Blissett. You don't know what Luther Blissett is? Luther Blissett is a collective name, a communal name — anyone can sign their name that way—artists, hackers. Anybody can be Luther Blissett. It's like saying no one.

Grazia jumped up from where she was sitting and brushed off the seat of her pants. Matera and Sarrina were coming toward her with Rahim, a twenty-one-year-old Tunisian, illegal alien, drug dealer. They had taken him into an alleyway behind the theater to interrogate him—he wouldn't have talked in front of Grazia. She had been waiting a long time and was impatient. She knew, as soon as she saw Sarrina shake his head, that they hadn't gotten anything out of him. Matera glared at Rahim one last time before letting him go, pointing at him without a word, the way the police do when they have nothing left to ask but they're still not satisfied with what they've heard.

When the sun goes behind the buildings, when it gets so low it seems to have gone underground, then the streetlamps in Piazza Verdi come on. At first, when they're warming up, the light they give off is opaque and pallid and stays high up in the globes, practically sticking to their sides. It doesn't reach under the porticoes. Shadows are gloomy there, and faces are dark.

Trust me, Matera had said—this city isn't like others.

Some Venetians have a singsong way of speaking. I think of it as singsong because their voices go up and down as if they're following the rhythm of a song. Up and down, up and down, their voices intone their sentences, starting off high in the back of their throats and ending through their noses, distractedly, like a tune being sung absentmindedly or hummed. Then, just as the sentence is about to end, it's as if they remember the rhythm, so they add a final twist that folds back on itself.

"Ma va' in mona! Lo sapevi che la macchin me serve perche' xe lo sciopero dei treni e allora come ghe torno a ca'?" ("What the hell! You know I needed the car because of the train strike, now how am I going to get home?")

The people that live in the region of Lombardy, the Bergamascans, for example, have a returning inflection. I call it returning because they, too, end their sentences with a twist, but it's longer, harder, more drawn out. They end their sentences in the same hurried, loud way that they begin them, only with a slight kick on the penultimate syllable, which leaves the whole rest of the sentence sort of hanging in the air.

"Senti'! La macchina mi servi-iva a me' e allora? E vienici

anche te a senti-ire i Soundga-ar-den, no?" ("Hey! I needed the car too, alright??? Why don't you come to the Soundgaarden concert, too, OK?)

People from Emilia Romagna have a slippery way of speaking. They open their vowel sounds wide, so they can slide across them, so they can stretch and push them out of shape from the inside, the way your fingers move through cake dough, twirling it, letting it twirl around you. If they're from Parma, they roll their Rs, if they're from Modena or Carpi they might end their last syllable with an O sound, hard and tight.

"Eh, soccia che marraglio . . .adesso mi chie-edi i biglietti per i Soundgaaarrrden? Eh fiiiga!" ("Hey, what a frigging pain . . . you're asking me for Soundgaarden tickets now? Well screeeeww you!)

Ligurians speak with a river current accent. I call it that because, often, at the beginning of their sentences, they take a breath before letting the words flow out one after another, until all of a sudden they're at the end of the sentence, when they raise and drop the final vowel sound as if it were two separate notes.

"Eh, beli'n! E devochiederallaradioibigliettandcheperte'-e??" ("Oh right! sonowIhavetoasktheradioforticketsforyou-toohuh–u??)

A Roman accent is made up of broken sounds. They break up the words in different places and in different lengths, sometimes short and sometimes long. They let the sounds hang out of their mouths, teeter on their lips, sort of like a wooden match when it breaks in half, but not all the way.

"A Marcoooo! Che stai a di'? La macchina 'ndo' sta?"
("Oh! Marcooooo! whatcha'doin? Where'sa car?")

Singsong, broken, sliding: the voices of the city come out the speakers of my scanner and swirl around me. They mix together, blend and wash over me like water going down the drain with me in the middle—me, on the swivel chair being spun around myself, the words spinning around me, faster and faster and faster.

The last page was a sheet of lined, pale gray, size A4 paper. It had perforated edges from a continuous traction bubble jet printer. At the top of the page it had the seal of the Republic of Italy. Under that it read:

TRANSCRIPTION OF THE CROSS-EXAMINATION OF LORENZO DEIANNA: SUSPECTED OF MULTIPLE CHARGES.

"Bingo!" Vittorio had scrawled across the top of the page.

Assistant Procuratore Monti: Testing one two three . . . testing one two—does it work? Can I start now? OK. Today is March 17th, 1997. I, Patrizia Monti, Assistant Procuratore of the City of Bologna, together with Commissario Capo Vittorio Poletto of the Polizia di Stato will now proceed to cross-examine Lorenzo Dei-anna, age thirty-five, under investigation for the sexual assault of minors . . .

Deianna: Wait a second! You said we could forget about that.

Monti: Please, Signor Deianna, we've got to follow

procedure. We can discuss the plea bargaining later. As I was saying, under investigation for the sexual assault of minors, for exploitation of individuals by way of prostitution, for performing obscene acts in public, for violence to animals and for showing contempt to sacred objects. I hereby inform you that you have the right to remain silent. Will you make use of this right, Signor Deianna?

Deianna: Who, me? No way. That's why I'm here. We had an agreement, remember?

Monti: Agreement isn't quite the right word, Signor Deianna. Let's just say that we're gathering information in order to process your request.

Poletto: Excuse me, Counsellor. Do you think we can get to the point? I don't have much time.

Monti: Terribly sorry, Commissario, but we have to follow procedure—

Deianna: I must have met the guy three times, at the most. The first time was in September 1994, I think. He said he was interested in Satanism but you could tell right off that he wasn't all there. He was just one of those guys that likes to hang out with the sects. Jehovah's Witnesses, Sai Baba, any of them.

Poletto: What name did he go by?

Deianna: I can't remember. A normal name. Anyway, he came back a few months later and said he wanted to take part in a Black Mass. He said he needed to ask Satan something. We asked him for five hundred thousand lire, which is the going rate. He gave us a hundred thousand as down payment and for initial purification rites. Two nights later, we were at Armarolo di Budrio, an old, abandoned villa, with five or six other novices who had paid for a Mass with virgins and the sexual rites, but this guy doesn't show up. I swear I didn't know that the girl was a minor, your Honor! I swear I didn't touch her!

Monti: Signor Deianna, the girl says you drugged her and that you —

Poletto: What did he need to ask Satan?

Deianna: Who?

Poletto: The guy. You said he needed to ask Satan something. What was it?

Deianna: Ummm, I don't know, I didn't really get it, you know what I mean? It was something weird. He wanted to ask him to please stop ringing the bells.

In the margins Vittorio had written in capital letters:
"SAI BABA, JEHOVAH'S WITNESSES . . . AND THE BELLS. HE WANTS SATAN TO STOP RINGING THE BELLS."

Vittorio had written more notes on the back of the page. His handwriting was hurried but small and tight. His lines slanted toward the bottom of the page. In some places, the soft lead of his Pentel pencil had smudged and faded slightly. Occasionally words had been erased.

"That's it. That's what he's running away from. That's what scares him. That's the sound he hears, the sound he tries to cover up with headphones, that he mumbles to himself, like someone who can't get a tune out of their head. BELLS.

"Satan's bells. And do you know what bells signify, Ispettore Negro? Do you know, in psychoanalysis, what the dark cavity and the clapper signify? Do you know what the undulating rhythm of bells represents? (You're turning red, aren't you, sweetheart?)

"They're the bells of sin. Death bells. The bells that ring when you die.

"Our Iguana doesn't want to die—he's afraid of going to hell.

"So what does he do, sweetheart?

"He reincarnates.

"The Iguana hangs around religious sects, but only those that believe in reincarnation! That's what happens when he kills someone, but in his own way. And faster, without a whole life cycle taking place. He takes off his clothes and draws a mask of circles on his face, like the Maori warriors' tattoos. He changes skin like an Iguana from the Galapagos. Like a primitive man or a dinosaur or a dragon—ready to transform into a more evolved form.

"His victims have to be young because the Iguana doesn't believe in senescence. He denies his own sexuality, which makes him afraid. He denies death. He wants to be *immortal!*

"Or maybe he's just trying to become great in some way."

Then, farther down, squeezed into the bottom of the page, more writing. Ball-point pen. Red ink.

"Isn't it absurd, Ispettore Negro?
We know all about him but it doesn't matter.
Who is he now?
What is he doing?
What does he look like?"

Please stop ringing, bells, especially now that I have to take off my headphones—

Please—

You won't, will you?

I suppose I'll have to turn up the stereo—who cares if the speakers explode in my face? Nine Inch Nails: *Mr. Self Destruct*. The sound of a sledgehammer beating against steel, pounding hard and fast as if it's trying to break through something. Each blow sets off a liquid vibration, as if the hammer were right here, pounding on the wet floor of this bathroom. When the music explodes into scathing distortion, it's as if thousands of crazed fingernails are scratching at the condensation around me, as if dishes are being thrown against the wet, slippery tiles of the walls. Amid these explosive sounds, a calm voice intones. *"I am the voice inside your head, I am the lover in your bed, I am the sex that you provide, I am the hate you try to hide . . . and I control you."*

I wipe away a circle in the fogged-up mirror with the palm of my hand, round and round, until I can see my reflection. I have to look quickly, because the steam from the hot water taps of the sink, bathtub, and shower that I have running will fog it up again. The scabs on my head are almost completely healed; if I pick them, they'll come off easily, leaving smooth, pink skin. But the scabs on my chest and thighs haven't dried up yet, so I leave them alone. The scabs between my legs hurt. The blade was rusty. I'm not used to shaving myself down there.

Nine Inch Nails: "Heresy."

It also starts with the sound of a hammer pounding on a watery surface. This time the voice screams gutturally. "*Your God is dead and no one cares, if there's a hell I'll see you there.*"

Stop ringing!

I wipe the condensation off the mirror again and look at myself closely, first at one side of my face and then the other. The safety pins that I stuck through my earlobes, nostrils, and eyebrows hurt, but not too much. I couldn't find anything else in the house to use to pierce myself with; the earring posts were too thin and not sharp enough. But the safety pins worked well— now all I have to do is grab the skin around my eyebrow, lift it up a little, ouch, extract the safety pin, oucchh, open the hoop, slide one end in and push it through owww! Then I rotate it, carefully, without moving my eyebrow or blinking or else it hurts even more. Big red drops of blood fall into the sinkful of hot water, spread across it, dissolve, then flow over the rim. I do the same thing to the left eyebrow, but it's harder because I'm right-handed. It makes me nauseous. I scrape the bone with the metal of the earring, but I keep pushing. My wrist is killing me, but finally the earring pokes through. It doesn't hurt as much to do my ears. I barely feel my nose at all.

Suddenly, my face feels on fire. I splash cold water on it. I turn my back to the mirror and lean my butt on the sink. I can't even think about the last earring. I just have to do it. I know it's there, between my legs. If I look down I can see it. It's throbbing, red and swollen. It looks like a skewered fish.

Nine Inch Nails: "I Do Not Want This."

The singer howls from some underneath place, from underwater or from beneath the skin. It sounds like there's a membrane of cellophane wrapped around him. "*Don't you tell me how I feel, you don't know just how I feel . . .*"

Oh God! It hurts! It really hurts!

I double over and fall to my knees. The pain shoots through my stomach, it takes my breath away. It hurt less when I stubbed out the cigarette on my thigh—the smell of burning skin, the sound of searing flesh, and the scorching feeling made me wince, but it didn't hurt as much as this. There's at least an inch of water on the tile floor, but it's cold. It makes me shiver. The hot water faucets are running and there's a lot of steam, but I still feel cold. It's like this each time I reincarnate. I'm cold and naked.

Clang, clang, clang . . .

Suddenly, the cell phone on the bathroom shelf rings. It feels like someone is scratching their fingernail up the back of my neck. I reach up and answer it.

"Hello?"

"It's me — Paola — is that you, Vopo?"

"Yeah."

"You sound weird. What's all that noise? Are you taking a shower with the radio on?"

"Sort of."

"Hey, what's going on . . . are you fucked up? Listen, fuckup, everyone's getting together tonight at the Teatro Alternativo. Mauro's playing in a jazz band. You want to come?"

"Yeah, I'll come."

"You sure? You'll remember?"

"Yeah. Tonight. Teatro Alternativo. Fine."

Nine Inch Nails: "Reptile."

"Angels bleed from the tainted touch of my caress, need to contaminate in order to alleviate this loneliness . . . my disease, my infection, I am so impure. . . ."

I put the phone back, wipe off the mirror with both my hands, and watch my reflection slowly disappear. The animal slithers through me, distending my stomach. It writhes up my chest, around my throat, under the skin of my face, cheekbones, and eyes. It pushes against my mouth, making my lips curl out. If I open my mouth I wonder if I'll see it but I'm scared, so I don't. I swallow it instead, forcing it back down my throat. I take a breath of the hot, steamy air.

I check my reflection against the picture ID card propped against the mirror, even if it's small and hard to see, but it's better than looking at the body floating in the bathtub, arms and legs hanging limply over the rim. It has no skin left on its face. On the ID card I can see the shaved head, the bags under the eyes, the puffy lips. I remember where he had worn earrings, because I'd yanked them out. You can still see the hairless chest and legs and the scar on the thigh on the body in the bathtub.

I look at myself in the mirror again.

We look exactly the same.

But the bells are still ringing. I'm still hearing them—

Climbing the stairs to Simone's room, Grazia noticed the variety of sounds that came from behind his door. Like market day in the piazza, only quieter. Like she was about to step into an invisible street where people, cars, scooters, distant music, and sirens all carried on, but in a whisper. And yet behind the door was only his room, his attic, a rectangular bedroom with exposed beams, a sofa, and three small skylights. Chet Baker was playing on the stereo. Simone was sitting on the edge of his swivel chair, his elbows on the desk, chin in his hands. Eight scanners were on at once, all picking up sounds, all at less than a third of their potential volume.

Simone was humming to himself. Not "Almost Blue." He was humming "Summertime."

"What's up? Are you happy?"

"No."

Simone pushed his chair away from the desk and sat up. He started to rock back and forth, his toes pushing off the floor, slowly and rhythmically. Grazia realized that she had made him blush, and smiled.

"Me neither. I've been all over the city and still haven't found out what I wanted. I'm tired. Do you mind if I stay here for a while and watch you? I mean, it's not like you're our only hope, but even so . . ."

Simone shrugged and turned back toward the scanners, as if he wanted to crawl into the jumble of wires and voices. Grazia sat down on the sofa, took off her jacket, and leaned back on a pillow with a sigh. She watched him carefully. His dark brown hair was tied back, no special way, just to keep it off his face. His mouth was closed. One of his eyes was always half-shut, making his face look asymmetric, almost crooked. Grazia watched him adjust the dials on the scanners, changing frequencies with slight movements of his thumb.

—"This is Siena Monza 51, I'm on my way to . . ."

—"Francesca, where the hell are you? I've been waiting for an hour . . ."

—"Come in — Mephisto — this is Satan, I'm passing through the Modena tollbooth . . ."

—"Hold on, I want to let this car go by . . . I'm in Forli, I don't know which road to take . . ."

—"No trouble at all . . . I'm on the train, on the way to Imola to see . . ."

"How can you follow them all?"

"I don't follow them. I just listen. I'm listening for the voice."

"Are you sure you remember what it sounds like?"

"Yes."

"Sorry, what I meant was: What did it sound like?"

"It was green."

"Green?"

"Cold, fake, tight—as if he had to hold it back or it would slip off his tongue. As if he were hiding something."

"Why green?"

"Because of the *R* in green. Because green is a rough, grating word and I don't like rough things. It was an ugly voice. It was a green voice."

"Oh. What color is my voice?"

Simone bit his lip and leaned toward the sea of voices. Before he immersed himself in the sounds again he said, "Blue," but said it so softly and quickly that Grazia couldn't have possibly heard him.

—"Telecom Italia Mobile. The person you are trying to call is momentarily . . ."

—"Omnitel. We are now transferring your call. Please stay on the line . . ."

—"Telecom Italia Mobile. The number you are trying to call has been changed or disconnected. Please check the number . . ."

"Do you mind if I take off my shoes? I took a shower this morning so I don't think they'll stink but I've been running around . . ."

Grazia took off her sweatshirt, sniffed it, and shrugged. She rapidly touched herself between her legs, on the rough seam of her jeans, trying to remember if she had put a tampon in that morning, as she was practically at the end of her cycle. Then she moved to the edge of the sofa and began untying the laces of her sneakers.

Chet Baker's voice came from the stereo.

The acute whistle of a fax machine came from the scanners. The rough crackle of a cell phone with a dead battery. The synthetic notes of Ravel's *Bolero* on an answering machine.

Chet Baker's trumpet.

"What's wrong?" Grazia asked in alarm. Simone had turned toward the wall, his head cocked to one side as if searching for something. He relaxed as soon as he heard her speak, and turned his face back to her.

"Nothing," he said. "I just couldn't hear you anymore."

"I'm right here," Grazia said, and came over to stand behind him. Simone shifted uncomfortably in his chair. He began to rock back and forth again, slowly and nervously. Grazia moved closer and placed her hand on the back of the chair to stop it from swaying. She sat down gently on the armrest, one hand on the table for balance. Simone's nostrils flared. He moved away slightly, as if embarrassed.

"Oh, I know . . . I told you I've been running around all day."

"No," he said swiftly, "it's not that." He raised a hand as if to silence her. "That doesn't bother me. But there's a smell I don't recognize. Something oily."

Grazia reached back to the holster hanging from her belt.

"My gun," she said.

"Oh, right."

Simone tipped his head toward Grazia. His nostrils flared again

"Rubber. You're wearing sneakers."

"Yes. Don't embarrass me, OK?"

"Smoke."

"Yes, but not mine. It gets absorbed by my jacket. Matera and Sarrina both smoke."

"Your skin smells strong, a little bitter. There's the smell of a warm, heavy fabric and maybe a cotton undershirt. And then there's something acidic, almost sweet, but less than the first time you were here."

"Now you're making me uncomfortable."

"The smell of 'Summertime.'"

"Holy shit! You're right."

Grazia sang the first notes — *da da dummmm* — off key and rushed. Without thinking, she pushed the chair off the ground with her foot, making it rock. Both of them smiled.

"Practically the only reason I bought it was because of the song in the advertisement. Incredible, Simone, you're like the guy in that movie. Did you —"

She had been on the verge of saying *see it* but stopped and bit her lip. Simone shook his head and kept smiling.

"No," he said, "I don't go to the movies too often."

Grazia smiled. She liked his asymmetrical expression, the way he couldn't stare at her, the way he couldn't ask anything of or about her with his eyes. She realized that the sense of relief she had felt as soon as she walked in was not because she could finally sit down, but because of him. She could talk to him without his ogling or inspecting her. He couldn't ask her to do things with his gaze: "dress like a woman"; "stay here and work with me"; "get him, sweetheart." Simone didn't do that, he wasn't ironic or patronizing. He didn't want anything. He just listened.

"Besides the movies, Simone, what else do you do?" she asked, in as gentle a voice as she could manage.

"I listen to the voices on my scanner."

"What else?"

"That's all."

"Don't you ever go out? You must go out some-times—"

Simone stopped smiling. He leaned forward into the web of wires, fingering the dials as if they were piano keys.

"No," he said.

—"That's fine with me. Let's meet at ten at Paradise . . ."

—"Manu's going to meet us at the rest- . . ."

—"Tell me where we can find . . ."

—"It's me—Paola—is that you Vo—"

Me neither, Grazia thought to herself. Except for pizza or a movie once in a while with a girlfriend who works in the immigration office, but that doesn't really count.

"You see other people, don't you Simone? I mean friends, or something?"

"No."

—"Listen fuckup, everyone's getting together to-night . . ."

Me neither, Grazia thought. Except for Vittorio and a couple of acquaintances from various professional training courses, but they don't count as real friends.

"Do you have a girlfriend?"

"No."

Simone leaned even deeper into the buzzing voices, then turned his head toward his left shoulder.

"What about you?" he asked softly.

Grazia shook her head.

"Me? No. Not now. I have a lot of work. . . . What's the matter?"

Simone shifted in his chair so suddenly that Grazia's leg slipped off the armrest. He'd turned his head to the right toward the scanner and reached out and squeezed her arm so hard it hurt.

—"Yeah, I'll come."

—"You sure? You'll remember?"

—"Yeah. Tonight. Teatro Alternativo. Fine."

The click of interrupted communication. The sound of the empty airwaves. Simone turned off all the scanners except for the one at the far right.

A wrinkled, green buzzing sound.

Grazia rushed over to the bed, where she had left her bomber jacket. She took out her cell phone and quickly dialed a number, at the same time wiggling her foot into one of her sneakers.

"Matera?" she said, almost shouting into the phone, then pointed her finger at Simone, "We're breaking the rules tonight. We're going out. You and me."

The surface underfoot feels soft and thin and has sticky ridges: a rubber mat on a cement ramp. I feel the cool, open air of evening around me. It gets warmer as we climb toward the entrance. The doors are wide open. I hear a distant sax but it's muffled by the sound of people around me, by the noise of the traffic in the street and by a single loud voice at my lower left ("Can I see your ARCI card? Ten thousand lire to get in.") We're at the Teatro Alternativo on Via Irnerio.

Now the ground is flat cement. I shuffle along until I discern a step in front of me. There's always one of these steps at this kind of entrance but Grazia doesn't notice it and she stumbles, grabbing at my arm for support.

"Sorry," she mumbles. "Come on—Matera's over there."

Inside there's the smell of smoke, both the dry and the sweet kind. I can smell heat, dusty cement, damp plaster, and sour paint. Paper. I run my finger against the wall and feel the wallpaper. The smell of wine. The bitter smell of beer. A strong, fleshy smell comes from the floor. I tug on Grazia's arm; she's guiding me.

"What? Damn, I almost stepped on a dog. It's so dark

in here—you can probably find your way better than I can."

I bang my hip on something hard. It's wet and smooth and has rounded edges. I slip my fingers underneath. It's deeper than my arm is long. The smell of wine. The bitter smell of beer. It's the counter of the bar.

"Good evening, Signor Martini," Breather says, his gruff voice exhaling old tabacco in my direction. I feel his hand on my shoulder but his voice goes in another direction. He's whispering but I can hear him.

"There's no backup, Ispettore."

"Christ, Matera!"

"You know where we are, don't you? Do you know why it's called the Teatro Alternativo? This place is run by the Autonomi. The questore decided not to give us a backup because whenever the cops come here, all hell breaks loose."

"Fuck, Matera! The Iguana's here tonight!"

"The questore doesn't believe that the Iguana exists. Anyway, no backup. It's you, me, and Sarrina, who's already inside, over there, behind the curtain."

Grazia squeezes my arm, then leans over and whispers something in my ear, her mouth almost touching my skin. I have to pull up my collar to hide the shiver that runs through me. She's guiding me toward the thick, rough curtain that muffles the trumpet sound that is getting closer and closer.

"Don't be scared," she says, "we'll look for a guy with headphones, I'll bring you up to him, and Sarrina will get him to say something. If you recognize his voice,

Matera and I will nab him and take him outside. Just stay calm. It's not dangerous. He won't even notice you. It's just a question of finding a guy with headphones . . . oh, shit!"

Grazia lowered her arm, letting the heavy curtain that separated the theater from the foyer brush against her cheek. She blinked several times to get used to the dim light, but she had already noticed them. Three guys were standing under the blue light of an exit sign to her right. One was leaning against the wall on her left, cast in the fluorescent light that came from the bathroom door. Two girls were standing in front of the sound mixer. Behind them, at the bar, another guy was leaning against the posters on the wall, a joint in his hand. The third was petting the dog, a graffiti banner sprayed onto the wall behind him. All of them were wearing headphones. They wore them around their necks or they held them in their hands; wires hung down their shirts or vanished into their pockets.

"We're screwed," Sarrina said to her. "The movie theater around the corner is showing a foreign film festival. They have a simultaneous translator. But the film tonight wasn't any good and a lot of them came over here to check out the music but kept the headphones."

The Teatro Alternativo in Bologna is a small amphitheater. It has wide, cement steps that double as seats and lead down toward the stage. Except for the stage itself, which is lit by spotlights, and for some dim lights above the columns in the walkway around the back of the theater, it's completely dark. Only blurred shapes, vague outlines, and movement are visible. Despite the palpable darkness, which doesn't get any lighter even as your eyes adjust to it, it's always crowded, just like every club in Bologna at night.

The band is good. The trumpet blows warm, round notes that pop over me like bubbles. I can feel the vibrations of the bass, chord by chord. There's even a piano; its sound tiptoes delicately down my back, as if it wants to slip unobtrusively away. The drums rattle so firmly I feel like I could lean on the sound as if it were a windowsill. The saxophone I heard earlier is obstinately quiet now.

Be-bop. A lively song, one I don't know.

I like it.

I feel like telling Grazia but I can tell how tense she is. Her breath is warm and damp, she's breathing hard. She squeezes my arm and pushes me forward.

"Fuck it. We'll get him anyway," she says.

"Hey, you got a smoke?

"No, sorry, it's my last one."

"Hey, do you know who these guys are?"

"Marco Tamburini and his new group. I know the sax player: Mauro Manzoni."

"Hey, what film was playing?"

"A classic, the restored edition of *Ugetsu Monogatari,* by Mizoguchi."

"You know where the bathroom is?"

"Over there."

"Where?"

"Over there. Can't you see the door?"

"Hey, aren't you Mirko's brother?"

"Me? No, why, do we know each other? What's your name? Hey, wait a minute, what's your name?"

"Excuse me, do you know what time it is?"

"What? It's hard to see, it's so dark . . ."

Holding on to her jacket, I follow Grazia through the crowd. Every now and then she stops and asks someone a question. I listen.

Yellow voice: acute and sticky. The syllables get stretched across each other.

Red voice: wide and full. Short and fat. Thick.

Orange voice: sour oranges when they sting the back of your throat.

Purple voice: saccharine and irritating, like a slight fever that doesn't go away.

Pink voice: soft and supple. From the back of the throat. Dripping from the lips.

I listen.

If it's not the green voice, I pull once on Grazia's jacket and we move on. If I can't tell, I pull twice and she asks another question. If it's him, I'm supposed to tug three times, quickly and firmly.

Red, blue, pink voices.

Orange, grey, brown voices.

Yellow voices. Purple voices.

Even some green voices.

But not his.

"You want some?"

Grazia stuck a bottle in Simone's face, who frowned, perplexed.

"Oh, sorry. It's beer. You want some?"

"No thanks."

"He might not be here yet. He might never show up. He might have been in the bathroom when we were in the hall or in the hall when we were at the bar or at the bar when we were in the bathroom. He might be standing by the stage, as quiet as a mouse. But if he's here, I'm going to find him. As soon as the show is over and the lights come on, I'm going to find him."

They were sitting on the ledge in the passageway at the top of the theater near the entrance curtain, leaning against the wall, backs to the stage. They weren't very comfortable, but they were tired of standing. Anybody coming or going had to walk in front of them. Grazia asked for a cigarette from every person that had on headphones, a Walkman, or even a hat. She had run out of questions. Simone listened. As soon as the person had gone by, she would stub out the cigarette on the wall and drop it between her legs. She didn't even smoke. When they sat down, Sarrina had come over and asked if she wanted a beer, but when he came back, he slipped it to her surreptitiously. "They've noticed us. One of the Autonomi we arrested at the Feltrinelli bookstore demonstration recognized Matera and me. We're going outside or else we're screwed," he had whispered.

"You sure you don't want some?"

"Yes, thanks. Really."

Grazia put her mouth on the bottle and tipped back her head. She took a long and frothy swig, wetting the corners of her mouth and drying it off with the back of her hand. She closed her eyes and leaned forward, elbow on her knee, chin in her hand. She was tired. And sweaty. She wanted to take off her jacket, boots, and jeans and jump in the shower. She wanted to feel the cool spray of water on her neck, tip her head first one way and then the other, let the water wash through her ears. She wished she was on vacation at her family's home in Lecce, at the beach. To sit on the warm sand, to look over at Simone sitting under the umbrella, to run down the beach to the water . . .

Simone. Usually, when her thoughts wandered toward the beach in Lecce, she saw Vittorio lying in the sun next to her, his arms folded behind his head. She had invited him down each time she had gone but he had always been too busy. So, instead, she imagined him there. Him watching her dig her feet into the sand, him turning over to look at her. But just now she had imagined being there with Simone. Simone, Vittorio. Why Vittorio? Why did she always have to imagine him? He wasn't there with her now. He was never there. Anger. She squeezed her eyes shut. Simone. Simone, next to her on the beach.

She breathed in deeply but, instead of salt air, she smelled the sweet smell of a joint. She opened her eyes and peered out into the dark, searching for an iguana with

a green voice and headphones. She took a swig of beer. It
ran down her chin. She leaned back and closed her eyes.

All of a sudden I hear it.

I didn't expect to, but suddenly, out of nowhere, I
hear that gentle, violet, resonating sound.

"Almost Blue."

It opens with a sax solo. I had forgotten about the
sax. It starts slowly and intimately, with a whisper. Then
the trumpet—modest and gentle—fills the sound the
sax makes, which, in turn, wraps around it like paper
around a gift, a blue gift.

Almost blue, there's a girl here and she's almost you . . .
Almost blue, almost flirting with this disaster . . .
Almost blue, there's a part of me that's only true . . .

I had never heard it performed live before, without
the veil of the speakers and the scratch of the needle. I
had never heard it so full. Beautiful, long notes that keep
changing and coming, one after another. I had never
heard it vibrate across or through my skin like this. I
bite my lip to keep it from trembling. I turn my head
away to hide my tears.

I had never heard music, really, outside of my room.
I like it so much, it scares me.

"Here," Grazia said without opening her eyes, feeling
Simone's fingers on the neck of the bottle, sliding down
toward her hand. She lifted the bottle toward him, but

his hand stayed where it was, on her hand. She smiled, put her beer in the other hand, turned her palm, wet and cool from the bottle, to take Simone's hand, knitting her fingers through his.

There.
The green voice. There.
It walks in front of me, whispering that sound, softly, but I can hear it and I know that's the voice.
the bells clanging, clanging . . .
I squeeze Grazia's fingers so hard, she gasps. She understands immediately.
"Where?"
"In front of me. He's walking by."
"Where, exactly? It's so crowded. To the right, to the left, where?"
"I don't know . . . he's not saying anything . . . to the left, I think."
"Which one is he? The short one? That tall guy? The blond one?"
"How do I know? I don't know which one!"
"Shit."
Grazia lets go of my hand. I hear her get up. I hear her moving away.
And then I don't hear her anymore.

Three people with headphones were in front of Simone. One was short and had the headset around his neck, backward, as if it was choking him. Another was tall and was wearing a ski parka, a red and white kaffiyeh, and a balaclava; Grazia could see the white wire trailing down one shoulder and into his coat pocket. The third person's head was shaved. He was wearing his headphones, but when he stopped to light a cigarette, Grazia noticed that he had three facial piercings—one in each of his eyebrows and one through his nose.

"Shit," Grazia said. She opened her jacket, extracted her gun, and holding it down by her leg, moved up behind them as they were exiting.

"Excuse me, can I ask you something?"

The boy with the ski parka looked down at Grazia's hand on his chest and glared at her, lowering his chin into his scarf.

"Why?" he asked. "What the hell do you want?"

"I just want to ask you a question. Could you come outside with me . . ."

"Why? Who the fuck are you? Hey, what the fuck do you want?"

She had taken his arm discreetly but forcefully, the fingers of her left hand pressing at his elbow, smiling in a way that was meant to look coy. He shook himself free.

"Who the hell are you? What the fuck do you want? Let go of me . . ."

"Hold on—wait a second—what's the matter? Let me have a look, I want to see your headphones. Matera! Sarrina!"

When she pushed the entrance curtain aside, he saw the gun.

"Hey! What's the gun for? Who the fuck are you, a cop?"

I hear people shouting.

I hear people moving on my left.

I get up and call out, "Grazia?" I reach out but Grazia isn't there . . .

I hear Breather saying, "Easy now, Kaffiyeh, or you'll get hurt."

I hear Small Change saying, "Calm down, everybody, just keep calm."

Then another voice says, "Bastard! Get your hands off!"

Then I hear a slew of other voices:

"What do you want? Leave him alone!"

"He's a cop! Shit, that guy's a cop!"

"They're arresting Germano! These shits are arresting Germano."

Chaos. The music stops. No trumpet, no sax. Just shouting, the rustle of clothing, and heels on the cement.

Then Grazia's voice: "Shit. They're not headphones. It's a hearing aid."

Why is that guy looking at me? What is he staring at?

He was sitting on the ledge with a girl and then, all of a sudden, he started staring at me straight in the face.

Who is he? I can't see him very well because it's dark, but I know he's looking at me.

He's watching me in a strange way. He's got his head tipped back and to one side. He's not staring at me, but toward me. Through me. Inside me.

I walk a little closer to see what he looks like. His eyes are closed. Even with his eyes closed I can tell he's staring at *me*. I know it, I just know it. I am absolutely sure that he knows who I am. He can see the shining dots that sting my face. He can see the slit in my skin on my forehead. He can see how my nose is deformed into a beak. He can even see the bells, Satan's bells, ringing in my head.

He keeps looking inside me. He can see the thing slithering under my skin, moving up and down my body. It pushes out my lips so I open my mouth and show him the animal. It opens its mouth too. It hisses at the man who can see into me with his eyes closed.

I bring my hands to my mouth and shove it back in, I force it down my throat. It hurts like hell, but I swallow it.

Then I escape. I drop my cigarette, step on it, and slip through the crowd toward an emergency exit.

But before I leave I take one more look at him. I want to see him up close. I want to see the man who can see into me with his eyes closed.

Who are you?

Who?

Who are you?

Part Three

Hell's Bells

My lightning's flashing across the sky
You're only young but you gonna die.
                            — AC/DC, "Hell's Bells"

il Resto del Carlino

(Bologna and Imola)

RECENT DEVELOPMENTS IN THE SEARCH FOR
THE MURDERER OF UNIVERSITY STUDENTS

Six students killed by one man

Victims found naked and mutilated
The police are searching for a man, code name *Iguana*

By Marco Girella

BOLOGNA — The police now have substantial evidence that could lead to the identification of the murderer of six university students. Unfortunately, the serial killer, known in code name as "The Iguana" and presumed responsible for taking six lives to date, is still at large in Bologna. After months of investigative research, the police are only now coming to grips with the atrocious truth: that one man is singlehandedly accountable for the gruesome massacre of six individuals. In what has come to be seen as some kind of ritual, the killer strips his victims and performs acts of violence on their bodies.

"The Iguana" kills remorselessly. He roams freely through the thousands of apartments that are home to this city's student population. To think that the police believed, until recently, that a different murderer was responsible for each of the victims, shocks beyond belief. There has been word of a special squad called in from Rome to assist the local Police. One certainty amidst much speculation: the hunt for "The Iguana" was formally announced last week when Police Headquarters handed over an identikit to the press (see insert), which they had originally labled as 'dangerous kidnapper.' It now seems that this indeed might be the face of the elusive "Iguana."

(p.2-3)

la Repubblica

Six students killed in five years

Maniac stalks students

A blanket of silence surrounds a city

By our correspondent
PIETRO COLAPRICO

BOLOGNA— Over the past five years, six university students have been brutally murdered here. Yet, day after day, the victims' relatives, friends and fellow students have kept surprisingly quiet about it, perhaps in the hopes of assisting the ongoing investigation or perhaps to ease their own suffering. However, it now seems as though they have actually been protecting the killer himself — "The Iguana" as he has been named by the Homicide Squad — allowing him to roam freely through the city, winning the confidence of young, unsuspecting students and leaving them, ultimately, naked and lifeless.

To this day, no official inquiry yet exists. Absurd as it may seem, the questore "neither acknowledges nor denies" the investigation. Security is tight; there are few leaks, and those that come forth speak of a world of sex and drugs, as if those two elements were substantial enough to explain the carnage that has taken place within the academic environment. One thing is clear: in their efforts to keep things quiet, the city of Bologna is as silent as a grave.

Il Messaggero

Il Messaggero

At first withheld, the truth leaks out
The shadow of a serial killer looms over the unsolved deaths of University students

by MARCO GUIDI

Finally, the investigation into the murder of six university students here alters its course. After numerous denials and conflicting stories, it appears as though the police have finally settled on what has come to seem to many as the most logical solution to this case: that the murders have been committed singlehandedly by a serial killer. The details of each homicide, the circumstances surrounding them and the gory uniqueness of the killer's method led most people here to fear this hypothesis long ago. Why it has taken so long for the authorites to accept it, we may only hope to one day discover. Only yesterday, as bluntly as they had originally denied it, the police publicly stated the new direction of the investigation. To top it off the inquiry has now been been honored with its very own code name: Operation Iguana, whatever that may mean.

(continued on page 19)

l'Unità

The Iguana Claims Six Victims

All bodies found naked; a possible witness

Three homicides, one killer. It seems as though one man is responsible for the death of six University students, brutally slain over the past few months. The elusive and dangerous figure known as "The Iguana" has all the characteristics of a serial killer. Although no official word prevails from the police or Procuratore's office —the case is enveloped in a shroud of silence—one is led to believe that the deaths, which until recently had been considered isolated acts of violence, are actually part of a large-scale, macabre mosaic. Indeed, the seemingly diverse episodes have two major elements in common: the alternative, somewhat bohemian lifestyle of the student victims and the fact that the victims were all found naked. Until recently, this last particular had been held back. It now seems as though there is an individual who may be able to assist the Police in their search for the Iguana, an individual who has seen everything, and who is now under constant police protection.

Stefania Vincentini

"You screwed up, sweetheart."

Grazia was sitting on the table at the forensic unit headquarters. She bit her lip, felt her throat tighten. She looked away from Vittorio and tried to hold back the tears. She kept her eyes focused on her boots, which she swung back and forth. She tried not to blink. She tried not to look at Vittorio. She didn't want to break down.

"The questore is furious. He couldn't convince the newspapers that the serial killer doesn't exist. And he knows he'll have an even harder time with the students' mothers. Right now he's talking to a minister in the Justice Department. To tell the truth, sweetheart, I'm not too happy about it either."

Vittorio shuffled through some papers in his briefcase. He was standing in front of the window, his briefcase resting on the sill. He ran his finger along the diskettes that were tucked into the top portion of his briefcase.

"Yes, I wanted publicity, but not like this. Strategically speaking, the whole thing was premature. Now Alvau is struggling to decide whether to face the panic of an entire city or to continue the search for six separate killers."

He found the diskette he had been looking for, pulled it out, and tapped it gently against his furrowed brow.

"I almost had him," Grazia said, keeping her eyes to the floor. "I was so close."

Vittorio nodded. He slid the diskette into his coat pocket, then reached back into his briefcase and pulled out a comb. He looked at his reflection in the window and combed back his hair.

"I know. If the Iguana was there in the theater, you're the person who would have gotten the closest to him. But you jumped the wrong guy."

"Christ, Vittorio, you should have seen him! He looked exactly like him."

Vittorio put his comb away but kept smoothing back his hair near his temples. He looked at his reflection again and nodded, satisfied. He turned to Grazia, took her chin in his hand and tipped back her head so she was forced to look at him. Grazia bit her lip so hard she could taste blood.

"Look, I know how good you are. You found our only witness, you figured out that the Iguana changes skin, you thought of using the scanners to find him. That was great, sweetheart. You have good instincts; I like that in you. But I also know that you're young— and that I left you in charge of an investigation that's too much for you to handle."

Grazia tried to turn away, but Vittorio persisted.

"Our squad is so new, we're really still just a task force. But, one day, I'd like to see us develop into a fully operating unit, with our own specialists and investigations. To do that, we need a huge success, and the Iguana could have been it. I wanted you to bring me substantial proof and a clean investigation. You blew it. But it'll be all right. I'll take over now. I'll straighten things out."

"Do I have to go back to Rome?"

Although Vittorio was quickly disappearing behind a veil of tears, Grazia could see that he had turned back to the window and was smoothing down a stray lock of hair.

"No. Just lie low for a while until this all blows over. Don't let the questore see you. Your blind friend is leaving his deposition now, if they haven't already taken him home. Try getting something else out of him."

He chucked her gently under the chin.

"Chin up, sweetheart," he said, glancing at his watch. "Shit, in five minutes I have an interview with the television networks. After that, radio, and this is only the beginning." And then he left, remembering to lower his head as he passed through the low doorway. Grazia covered her face and started to cry.

Ouch. Suddenly, I feel pain. I bumped my leg on something hard. I almost lost my balance.

If I keep my hands down low, I can feel my way along the cold, smooth fenders of the car. I slide my hands along until I reach the end of it and then move carefully around it, limping slightly. I have to go very slowly. I feel lost and confused.

I know the courtyard of my building is small and square. I hear and feel the gravel underfoot. I know that farther ahead there's a smooth concrete sidewalk and steps that lead to the entrance of my building. But I didn't expect there to be a car here.

What if there's another one? What if there's a bicycle on the sidewalk? Or something on the ground?

I stand still and listen.

Traffic, coming from the street beyond the courtyard.

I smell the air.

A rotten banana from the dumpster on my left.

I step away from the car. The gravel crunches. I stretch out my arms in front of me and claw at the air. One step. Something moves in front of me, I shield my face with my arms, instinctively. Maybe it was just a fly. Now it's gone.

Another step.

And another.

My foot feels the sidewalk; I bend down to touch the ledge that runs along the wall. It's there. I lean on it with relief. Then I inch forward, my cheek brushing against the side of the building. I bang my hand on a windowsill that juts out; the pain shoots up to my elbow.

"Can I help you?"

A woman's voice, to my right. One hand touches my shoulder, then slides down my arm to my wrist. Her other hand holds my elbow, supporting me perfectly.

"Careful now, there are stairs ahead. It's all right. Let me help you . . . I'm used to it. My son is blind too."

I let her guide me.

I only wanted to see if I could cross the courtyard with my eyes shut, like I saw him do when I followed him home the other night. The man that can see through me. Now I'll have to keep them closed even though it's starting to tickle.

"I came down to wait for my son. He should be here any moment," the woman said. "It's a pleasure to help you. My son's name is Simone. Do you know him?"

"Simone?" I ask, reaching out to feel the door that she's holding open for me. "I know him very well. Actually, I came to see him."

"Simone Martini? The blind guy? He left about fifteen minutes ago. Castagnoli took him home when his shift was over."

The officer at the reception desk stared at her. He was leaning back in his chair, with one knee bent against the desk and his elbows on the armrests. Grazia rubbed her moist cheek.

"Could you do me a favor? Could you call the Martinis' house and let them know I'm on the way?"

"Sure — only I can't do it until this red light goes off . . . all the lines are busy."

Grazia dug her hands into her pockets and leaned against a cabinet. She stared at the ground. She felt the officer's eyes on her.

"Bad cold, huh?"

"Yes."

"You want a tissue?"

"No."

There was a battered portable radio on the desk. Its antenna was bent and short. Static distorted the voice coming from the speaker. The officer yawned. When he leaned forward and touched the antenna, the words come through comprehensibly, although they still sounded flat.

—R: Let's ask Dottor Poletto, director of the police unit that deals expressly with serial killers.

"Damn foolishness," the officer said and lifted his finger off the antenna. Thick static covered Vittorio's voice. The officer touched the antenna again.

"Can't do this all day," he said, lifting his finger slowly off the antenna. The static was less insistent.

—P: We're following several different leads right now. My personal opinion is that the Iguana exists. And that we'll catch him.

—R: What was the motive behind the arrest of the young Autonomo? Do we have another Carlotto case on our hands? Does this constitute political stereotyping? Is it a political gesture?

—P: Thank you for asking that question. This has nothing to do with the Carlotto case; the Autonomo has already been released. It was purely a mistake. One of our younger detectives acted on impulse.

"Sure," the officer said ironically, picking up the handset of the telephone. The red light had turned off.

"That's what they always say. They send in the young guys so that later they can put all the blame on them. What's the number?"

Grazia told him. She kept her eyes on the floor. She tried not to listen to Vittorio's voice; the radio was frizzing again and the officer was talking on the phone.

—P: If that's what the judge decides, then so be it. I'm ready to intervene and take over the investigation myself. But it's not up to me to decide.

"Hello, is this the Martini residence? Police head-quarters. Ispettore Negro would like you to know that she will be coming over shortly to talk to . . ."

—P: Yes, that's right, we're a task force. However, I am highly convinced that now is the time for . . .

"Well, I suppose it'll take about twenty minutes, but I can't be sure. There might be traffic. In any case, she'll be there soon."

—P: Why "Iguana"? It was a hunch, you see . . . I had been thinking about . . .

"No problem. Have a nice day."

Her arms crossed in front of her, Grazia narrowed her eyes and clenched her teeth. Her eyelids itched. *Don't worry, sweetheart. I'll take over now.* Right.

"The blind guy isn't home yet," the officer said. "They're worried because it's taking so long. I'm not surprised—he's so weird! Anyway, I told the guy not to worry, that . . . hey! what the . . . ?"

Grazia had turned suddenly toward him, pushing the desk roughly, making the officer's chair tip precariously backward. Vittorio's voice vanished into a violent crackle of static.

"You told the guy? *What guy?*"

"How the hell do I know?"

"Who was on the phone?"

"How the hell do I know? A man, a kid. Shit, Ispettore, someone who was there."

The sweet smell of lemon, the tangy odor of a cleaning liquid. The upholstery in the backseat is soft. My hand sticks to it. Brigadiere Castagnoli must have recently washed his car.

I hear the drone of the engine. It increases as we speed up, but then it quiets down. I don't like traveling by car. It's like moving while standing still.

"Don't you have a radio?" I ask, but he doesn't understand what I mean because I hear him press a button and the greenish sound of the news washes over me. Don't like it at all.

—R: Joining us today is Dottor Poletto, director of the Unit for the Analysis of Serial Crimes.

"No, I mean a police radio. Doesn't this car have one?"

"No, not this one. It's not a squad car. This is my car. I just ended my shift; your house is on my way home. But I do have a CB—I'm a radio buff. Is that OK?"

No, not really. I wanted to hear a real police radio. Without a scanner. Live, like music. I would have liked to reply to somebody's call, knowing that somewhere out there someone was listening.

"Damn traffic," Castagnoli mumbles, passing me the CB transmitter. "It's red again."

Grazia leaned forward and grabbed the siren from under the passenger seat. She propped it on her knees. With one hand she lowered the window, with the other she plugged the jack into the cigarette lighter. She clamped the flashing blue light onto the magnetic plate on the roof of the car just as they lurched forward, jolting her back into her seat.

Matera peeled out of the Piazza Roosevelt parking lot, hit 110 kilometers per hour on Via Zecca, then braked suddenly, downshifted, and turned onto Via Ugo Bassi, leaving the sound of the siren behind them. He changed gears quickly, with brief, smooth movements, the seat belt tense against his bulky body. Grazia, who had not yet fastened hers, was thrown back and forth between the door, the dashboard, and the seat, the buckle still in her hand. She dug her boots into the floor and pushed as far back into the seat as she could only an instant before Matera slammed on the brakes behind a bus, then swerved to overtake it, almost brushing along-side it. He cut back in front of the bus and turned sharply down Via Marconi. The driver of the bus, who was bald and had a short beard, honked vehemently, his lips moving rapidly in a string of obscenities.

Grazia clenched her teeth, pushed herself back into the seat, grabbed onto the handle above the door and directed the seat buckle to the clasp. She had forgotten how it felt. How her skin burned with the rush of adrenaline. She kept her eyes focused on what was in front of them. The cars vanished as quickly as Matera turned the steering wheel to overtake them. Pedestrians froze to let them pass. She looked out the window, unable to think clearly. Nine times out of ten, when they had been called in on a burglary, they'd receive the all-clear signal just as they reached the location. The release of tension was exhausting in itself. She wished for an all-clear signal now, too. A voice on the radio say-ing everything was all right, that Simone was safe, not to worry.

"Shit!" Grazia exclaimed when Matera had to brake because of a traffic jam. "You knew there'd be traffic on the Viali!"

Matera didn't say anything. He downshifted, the motor straining hysterically, turned into the emergency lane, and stepped on the accelerator.

A siren is approaching us from behind. It passes alongside, then moves on with that horrible yellow scream that always gives me goosebumps.

"Damn, he's going fast!" Castagnoli says, honking twice. "Slow down—you'll get there!"

At the stoplight on Via Costa the traffic was so backed up the cars couldn't maneuver to let them through. On the other side of the intersection, Grazia saw a truck trying to turn around, so she unfastened her seat belt, pushed aside the siren wire, and jumped out of the car.

She started to run, her boots pounding against the sidewalk. She pushed off with the tips of her toes to go faster; her hands were clenched, her elbows and forearms rubbed against her sides. People stopped to watch her go by. She kept an eye on the building numbers— 11, 13, 15, 17—breathing hard—19, 21, 23—bent forward, lowered head—25, 27, and on. As she turned into the courtyard, she slammed her shoulder against the wall, almost losing her balance, but she caught herself on a car that had been parked there. She ran across the gravel to the front of the building, stopped, and leaned forward over her kees to catch her breath. She stood up, unzipped her bomber, and pulled out her gun.

The main door was ajar. She ran up the steps, pushed it open, and stepped inside.

The staircase led first to a mezzanine and then toward the back of the building.

She started to climb the stairs, still breathing heavily.

She kept the gun hidden behind her leg, in case some-one came out onto the landing.

The entrance to Simone's apartment was on the sec-ond floor. It had a wooden door and a brass nameplate above the bell. The door was slightly open.

Grazia ran her hand through her hair, pushing it off her damp face. Drops of cold sweat ran down her back, making her T-shirt stick to her body. She pushed the door open.

The hallway. At the end of it was the door to the staircase that led to Simone's room. Halfway down, on her right, was the kitchen. On her left was the door to the living room. All three of the doors were ajar.

"Simone?" Grazia called out, "Signora Martini?"

The door at the end of the hallway squeaked, then shut.

Click.

Grazia made her way down the hall with a lump in her throat. She kept the gun raised. She removed the safety. With a pounding heart, she opened the door.

The stairs to Simone's attic were narrow and steep. The brass banister ran along the wall. The bedroom door at the top of the stairs was closed.

Grazia turned on the light to see better, but the bulb in the sconce located halfway up the stairs flickered, then went out. She blinked her eyes in the darkness.

"Simone! Signora Martini!" she called out and began to climb the stairs.

From behind the door came the low hum of the scanners. Standing at the top of the stairs, looking under the doorway, Grazia could see a dark shadow. Suddenly, the shadow moved.

Grazia pointed her gun at the door, thumb over thumb, the way they had taught her at the academy.

"This is Ispettore Negro!" she shouted. "Police! Who's in there? Identify yourself. I'm armed and coming in!"

If Simone had been in the room, he would have replied by now. If Simone's mother had been in the room, she would have replied. But the shadow wasn't Simone's mother. The shadow wasn't Simone.

It was the Iguana.

Castagnoli was smiling; I can tell by the way his lips spread across his teeth.

"Of course, we could tune in to the police channel. But don't tell anyone or I'll get into trouble."

I'm smiling now, too. The thought of someone out there hearing me when I talk sends a shiver down my spine. I know I shouldn't say anything, that Brigadiere Castagnoli might get in trouble, but I can't resist the temptation. I press the button on the microphone so hard it crackles.

"Grazia? Are you there, Grazia?"

"Yes! I'm here!" Grazia called out.

To hear Simone's voice on the other side of the door, even though it sounded somewhat muffled, made Grazia cry out in relief. She lowered her arms, lifted her finger off the trigger, opened the door, and walked into the room.

"Simone! You scared the shit out of me!"

She tripped over something in the doorway and fell, losing her grasp on the door handle. Castagnoli's voice came through on the scanner: "No, Signor Martini! Give me the transmitter!" Grazia landed on the floor with a thud that knocked her momentarily senseless. Her gun fell out of her hand and slid across the slippery floor toward the blood-splattered wall, toward the stained curtains that fluttered wildly in the open window, toward the Iguana, who stepped on it with his bare foot. Grazia raised her head to look at him but at that very moment a draft blew the thin curtain over his face, veiling him in a shroud of rosy gauze. Grazia held back a scream. She saw a bloody, faceless, hairless, larvaelike figure. The thin curtain highlighted the bumps and ridges on his body—it was raised where he had earrings and it drooped into his eye sockets and nostrils, into his open, red mouth. Frozen in terror, she watched him bend down. She saw his face in relief. It looked like a cracked, clay mask. A mask of naked skin, glistening with clotted blood. She thought he had bent down to pick up the gun, but instead he had turned to look at her. He stuck out his tongue against the curtain, emitting a low noise that, though covered by the static from the scanners, sounded like a long, raspy breath.

Suddenly, the siren from Matera's car filled the court-yard and the vacuum of the stairwells. The Iguana turned toward the window, opened it, clambered up, and slipped out. Grazia would have scrambled out onto the roof to see where he was headed. She would have taken a shot at him. But as soon as she looked down and saw what she had tripped over coming in, she broke into a cold sweat.

"Mamma?" Simone called out from the bottom of the stairs. "Mamma?"

I hear Breather come rushing up the stairs behind me. He grabs me. I reach for the railing so I don't fall back. "Grazia?" I call out. I feel scared.

Breather moves past me and pounds up the stairs, his steps vibrating through the walls.

"Jesus Christ!" I hear him yell. So I follow him, fast. At the top of the stairs, Grazia's hands stop me. She blocks my way. "Don't go in! Don't go in!" she screams.

I can smell my mother's hair spray. And I smell blood. Lots of blood. I start to scream too.

"How's he doing?"

"I'm not sure. He doesn't say much. He speaks in one-word sentences. He cries a lot. I suppose you could say that he's behaving normally for someone whose mother has just been killed and who has to live under police protection."

"Snap out of it, sweetheart. It's nobody's fault. Not yours, or mine. It just happened."

It's strange. No matter what street you walk along in the center of Bologna, if you go one way, you always end up in Via Indipendenza. That's where groups of kids hang out on their *motorini* in front of McDonald's, where people meet and park their bicycles to go window shopping under the porticoes, and where buses pass noisily between them all. Even stranger: If you walk along those same streets in the opposite direction, they don't lead anywhere. To progressively smaller roads, until you turn a corner and they disappear altogether.

Vittorio checked his watch and nervously pushed back a lock of hair that had fallen out of place. He had bags under his eyes. Despite his tan, he looked pale, almost ashen. Grazia realized she had never seen him like this before. He always looked like he had just returned from vacation—relaxed and glowing. Impeccable. Above all, infallible.

But now he seemed different. He wasn't the same man that used to make her heart race. She remembered when they had first met, how he had stuck out his hand and said, "Welcome to UASC, Ispettore Negro," making her feel like Jodie Foster in *Silence of the Lambs*. This wasn't the same man who had caused her to blush when he first pronounced her name in a meeting. Not the same man who made her flutter inside when he called her "sweetheart." One night she had even dreamed of making love to him. The next day she couldn't stop blushing; she was sure he could tell what she had dreamed about. Now everything was different.

"Could I use your phone to call the pensione? I want to tell Sarrina that I'll be there soon."

"What's wrong with yours?"

"I forgot to charge it."

Vittorio put his hand into the deep pocket of his overcoat, took out his cell phone and handed it to her, then crossed over to the other side of the street. She dialed the number of the Pensione San Lazzaro where they were temporarily hiding Simone and asked for his room. The conversation was brief.

"It's me. I'm on my way," she said, then pressed the button to disconnect and waited for Vittorio to return from the newsstand where he had gone to ask for directions.

Some streets in the center of Bologna have multiple personalities; you notice them only when someone points them out to you. Under the porticoes of one street, for instance, there's something that looks like a window in the wall; it's covered with wooden shutters and iron grillwork. But if you push hard on the shutters, they open up onto a river, a kind of canal, with houses on its banks, their foundations eaten away by the damp and small rowboats tied to small moorings. Right in the center of Bologna. Right in the center of a very terrestrial city. Once you know about its existence, if you walk down the road and listen carefully, you can even hear the gushing river, a low growl strangled by a small dam. But if you don't know about it, all you hear is the sound of traffic on Via Indipendenza.

"I'm a psychiatrist, not a police officer," Vittorio said. "I know that serial killers get caught because they tend to hide their victims in places where they will eventually begin to decompose or because they let their victims get away or because they end up giving themselves away, haunted by a sense of guilt. But I really don't know how to catch them. I did everything I could to get this case and now that Alvau has decided to give it to us, I don't know where to begin." He smiled ironically. "You know what, sweetheart? More than wanting to catch the Iguana, I want to understand him."

"Not me. I want to get him. And Vittorio, don't call me sweetheart anymore. It bugs the hell out of me."

Vittorio tapped the antenna of the cell phone against his lips and narrowed his eyes, scrutinizing the sun as it went behind the porticoes. He didn't say anything, and neither did Grazia, who was thinking about Simone and the feelings she had experienced when she had held him in her arms on the threshold of his room. The feeling of wanting to cover him with her jacket and protect him. And there was an inner feeling of gentleness she had, a sensation she couldn't quite name and maybe never would. But it didn't matter. Grazia wasn't interested in naming things, not even understanding them. She knew what she wanted: to get the Iguana. And to be with Simone. She felt sad when he did and happy when he was.

Vittorio lowered the antenna of his cell phone and slipped it into his pocket. He glanced at his watch and shook his head.

"I'm late," he said. "Do you want a ride?"

"No thanks. There's something I have to do first."

"You're probably better off—I can't even remember where I parked the car. Some back road around here. Be careful, sweetheart . . . Grazia. The Iguana is naked and he needs to kill again. He took off his clothes in the attic because he was waiting for the blind guy. Go to the pensione, make sure no one follows you, and stay there, OK?"

She nodded.

"Ciao, sweetheart." Chucking her under the chin, he walked off.

Grazia watched him disappear around the corner and for the last time waited to see if she felt that strange fluttering inside. It was gone. She breathed deeply and crossed the street to the music store.

He looks younger on the news.

But that doesn't matter.

I watch him walk through the dark alleys and narrow streets. He looks up and down the rows of parked cars. He's getting nervous. Finally, he finds his car at the end of a dead-end street, practically buried under a wooden scaffold. I saw him park the car there earlier this morning when I began to follow him. I've been following him all day, waiting for that girl to leave. I don't like that girl; she scares me.

I'm following him now.

I follow at a distance so he doesn't notice me. I hide behind the columns of the porticoes. I squeeze between the gutter pipes, rusty and crusted over with pigeon shit. Then I catch up to him, I reach out and touch his shoulder.

He drops his keys.

"What the . . ." he starts to say, then stops and stares at me.

The first thing he notices are my headphones. He narrows his eyes. But then his eyes open wide in amazement when he sees the rest of me.

I'm naked.

Naked, with handcuffs on.

"Commissario Poletto?" I ask. He nods quickly. His hand moves toward the lining of his raincoat, then hesitates. He glances down the narrow street, observing the shuttered windows and empty porticoes, the abandoned raincoat and shoes that I removed a few steps back. Perhaps he sees the animal slithering under my skin, even though I'm trying to keep it from moving. No, he's staring at my naked, hairless body. He looks at my shaved head. He looks at the shiny earrings in my eyebrows, the headphones on my head, and at the cassette player that I stuck to my body with masking tape. He puts his hand inside his raincoat.

"I saw you on TV," I say. "I've come to turn myself in. I'm the Iguana."

He pulls out a small, black gun from his raincoat pocket and points it at me. He takes a step back and looks around as if he doesn't know exactly what to do. He seems scared so I raise my manacled wrists to reassure him.

"Don't move—or I'll shoot!" he says.

He kicks his car keys toward me.

"Open the door," he says. I kneel down, pick up the keys with both hands and open the back door. I climb in and slide my naked butt across the seat. He gets in next to me and locks the door with the remote on the keys but he's so nervous that he has to press it several times before he gets it right. Then he leans back against the car door and bites his lip. He keeps his gun pointed at me. He's holding it with both hands, and he's shaking a little.

"I don't want to hurt you," I say to him. "That's why I put the handcuffs on. I'm naked so you can see I don't have any weapons."

"Don't move. Just stay still. If you come toward me, I'll shoot."

I stay very still. I feel the animal moving around my stomach, so deep inside that he can't possibly see it. My nose bone throbs under my skin, but it doesn't pop out. The bells are far away, beneath the music on the Walkman. They clang behind my mouth.

"Answer my questions: Did you see me on TV?"

"Yes."

"Which news?"

"The one that starts at 1:30."

"Did you kill Signora Martini?"

"Yes."

"How?"

"I killed her."

"How?"

"I killed her. Why are you asking me how?"

"Because I need to be sure if you're the real Iguana and not someone pretending to be him."

"I'm not pretending. It's me. I'm the real Iguana."

He keeps staring at me. His eyes narrow and he bites his lip so hard that I see a blurred spot of red on his teeth. Maybe he just saw my nose move, pulling the skin across my cheekbones with it, making my skin wrinkle like the finger of a rubber glove. No, he can't have seen the animal. It's in my mouth. It's on my tongue. I hear its heart beating, beating like the bells.

"Why are you wearing headphones?" he asks, pointing the muzzle of the gun at my head.

"So I can't hear what's inside my head."

"What do you hear?"

"I hear bells."

He stops biting his lip. His eyes open wide.

"Christ!" he says and lowers the gun. But then he raises it again and slides farther back against the door. He's breathing heavily, his teeth are clenched, he's looking at me in a new way—he's still frightened but he's curious, too.

"All right," he says. "I believe you. You are the Iguana. I'm going to bring you in now. I don't know how, but I will. Christ, just stay still . . . stay still, now! Or I'll shoot."

Suddenly he shifts. I can see his finger on the trigger but I don't understand why. Then, under the sound of the music, I hear a light click and glance down at my Walkman.

The tape has gotten tangled and has automatically stopped.

At first my eardrums are still numb but when I fully understand that the music has stopped, the numbness fades quickly.

Those bells.

I bang my head against the glass window with each exploding peal: clang, clang, clang — they're getting louder.

"Stop! or I'll shoot!" he's yelling but I can't, and I

keep slamming my head against the glass until it cracks. I yank off the headphones, the bells are clanging even louder, so I start to scream. I cover my ears with my elbows because my wrists are locked up.

"Mamma! Mamma!" I scream.

"Stop! I'm going to shoot, you fucker!" he yells but he doesn't shoot. He's listening.

"Mamma! Mamma!" I keep screaming, elbows at my ears. "Mamma, the bells!"

"What bells? What are the bells like? Tell me! Christ! Autohypnosis!"

My eyes open wide. My eyelids curl back and my eyeballs puff up as if they're going to pop out of their orbs. They're being pushed forward by the tears that gush over my cheeks like a cracked aquarium. My upper lip droops down over my lower one, all the way down to my chin. My head drops forward onto my chest and my voice, squealing like a dolphin fetus, seems to come from a distant hole.

"Mamma! I hear the bells! Mamma!"

I'm rocking back and forth on the seat, arms up by my ears. Rocking back and forth, banging into the broken glass and the seat, shaking and shouting and clenching my teeth but the bells don't stop, they won't stop, they never stop.

His voice, distant now, pierces my brain.

"Stay still! Don't move. Tell me where you are. Who are you now? Who are you?"

I scream. My mouth swallows almost my entire face, thrusting my eyes against my forehead. My voice comes out swollen and distorted; it reverberates inside my throat as if it was a dark cave.

"—That kid freaks me out, Agata! He's abnormal! I don't want him in this house! It's him or me! It's him or me! Him or me!"

"Mammmmmaaaa!"

My mouth is closed, my lips peel back, my voice comes out in such a high-pitched, acute scream. The windows of the car explode in a cascade of white fragments.

"Why?" I hear him yell from far away. "Why don't they want Alessio? Don't move, don't come toward me or I'll shoot! Who doesn't want Alessio? Why?"

"The man is screaming at my mother. I'm in bed but I can hear them. He's shouting at her, "that kid's a pain in the ass! You're always saying 'be quiet or he'll hear us.' Be quiet or he'll hear us! You've got to get rid of him, Agata! It's him or me. I can hear him. You remember the other night? When we were screwing and he walked in in his T-shirt and underwear, shouting 'Mamma! I can hear the bells!' It freaks me out, Agata! That little kid, covering his ears, screaming and crying for you!"

I scream but my voice gets lost in the wildly pealing bells that break over the car, crushing the roof in on us. I want to get out, I want to get free.

"No! Don't move!" he shouts, but I raise my arms and knock the gun out of his hands with my fists.

Suddenly, my skin splits, it peels back over my bones like rubber and my nose pokes forward, pulling the rest of my face along with it. I lean toward him, and before he can move I shove my beak into his eye.

Afterward I realize that I've made a huge mistake. I wanted to turn myself in so that he would bring me to that blind man who can see inside me.

Now it's too late.

I look in his bag. I look for a note, a business card, an address. I riffle among his clothes and find a cell phone. As I'm pulling it out of his pocket I touch one of the buttons: The telephone turns on. A green light illuminates the mottled red interior of the car.

It automatically dials the last number he called.

A voice answers. I listen, then hang up.

I move into the driver's seat and turn on the lights because it's gotten dark outside. I still can't see anything, so I turn on the windshield wipers to clear away the thick red fog.

But the red fog isn't on the outside of the car.

It's inside.

Pensione Fiore San Lazzaro: How can I help you? Hello? Hello? Strange . . . they hung up.

"Summertime."

As soon as Grazia walks in the adjacent room I hear the song go through my head. I don't know if it's because I heard her footsteps or because I miss her smell so much. Either way, it covers up the smell of the dish of uneaten spaghetti that's on the floor next to me.

I hear her talking.

"Tell the concierge. Only people with authorization are allowed upstairs. There's a phone. They should call us when someone's on their way up—all right?"

I hear Small Change mumble in agreement. I hear him go toward the door in the other room and I hear the door close. Grazia sighs. I hear the bedsprings, as if she has sat down on the edge of the bed. I hear her undo her boot buckles. The shoelaces rub against the leather and slide through the loops. I hear the thump of her boots when she tosses them across the floor.

After taking off her boots, Grazia stretched, then reached behind her and undid her bra without removing her camisole. She was about to pull the bra straps through the armholes of her camisole when she glanced toward Simone's room and smiled to herself. One of the advantages to living with a blind person, she thought, is that you can get undressed without self-consciousness. She took off her camisole, her bra, and her jeans, but left her tights on. She hesitated, then put the camisole on again inside out. In the mirror above the dresser Grazia looked at herself. She ran her fingers through her hair. Even though she knew Simone wouldn't notice if she was in her underwear or if her hair was a mess, she wanted to look pretty. She frowned, then closed her eyes and smiled.

I hear Grazia coming toward me. Those are her stockings sliding across the carpet. That's her smell — oil, nylon, cotton, skin, and "Summertime."

She sits on the armrest of my chair. Her cool skin and scratchy stockings brush against my hand. I pull it away.

"You haven't eaten anything," she says.

"No."

"Aren't you hungry?"

"No."

"I brought you a surprise. Do you want to hear it?"

"No."

She gets up and puts something on the table. She unwraps an object covered in cellophane, the way my mother used to open a pack of cigarettes. I want to think about my mother, but I can't — yet. I've been avoiding thinking about her all day. Then I hear a different sound, which distracts me. I recognize it. It's a tape player, clicking shut.

A piano. One single, solitary chord. Then, the sound of the brush on the drums, like a gasp of air. One brief brushstroke. Piano, drops of water. A different, slower voice sings "Almost Blue." I've missed hearing it. God, how I've missed it. And Grazia too. But I'm scared. My mother is dead and this is not the "Almost Blue" I'm used to.

"They didn't have the Chet Baker version that you played for me," Grazia said. "Actually, they had a CD of it, but I only had a tape player. This is Elvis Costello's version. On the liner notes it says that *he* wrote "Almost Blue"— what do you think of that?"

"I don't read the liner notes. I just listen."

"Do you mind if I talk?"

"Yes."

"Do you mind if I stay here with you?"

"Yes."

"Why?"

"Because I want to be alone. In silence."

"Fine. Be alone. In silence."

Grazia turned off the tape player. She got up and went toward the other room but stopped in the door-way. She stood perfectly still, her arms folded across her chest, looking at him.

Simone sat perfectly still, one hand on the armrest, the other closed in a fist in his lap. His chin fell forward onto his chest, his mouth was closed in a childish pout.

One eye was closed, the other slightly open, giving him that asymmetric look.

Grazia stood so still it was as if she had ceased to exist, as if she had never existed. She watched Simone. She watched as he slowly raised his head as if to smell the emptiness and silence, now even void of the music. Finally he spoke.

"Grazia?" he whispered.

"Grazia?" he said again, anxiously this time.

"Grazia, where are you?" he said in fear. She rushed over to him.

All of a sudden she's next to me. I smell her perfume, the warmth of her skin in front of me, her lips on mine. I pull my head away, but she slides her hands behind my neck and pulls me to her.

I begin to tremble. I don't want to, but I can't help it. Her lips brush against me. When she sits down on my knees her fingers slip inside the collar of my shirt. She takes my hand and guides it under hers. I feel her warm, smooth skin.

She takes off her camisole. The smell of "Summertime" overcomes me. I can't feel anything else—just her breath and the way her stockings rub against me when she stands up to peel them off. I can't move. My hands are on her thighs. She takes my wrists and places my hands on the pink curve of her breasts and on the blue rise of her nipples. "Hold me," she says in a whisper. She lowers herself on me with a slow moan; I feel her surround me entirely—her smell, her warmth, the tangy, intense odor of her skin, the sweet heat of her shoulders and her breasts, the wet pressure of her mouth, her hot tongue across my lips, that electrical shiver I feel when our lips meet. She undoes my belt. She undoes my trousers. Her thighs squeeze mine; I feel the warmth of her body on my shorts when she rests on top of me as she leans back to remove my trousers.

"This is my first time," I mumble. I can hear her smile.

"Not for me—but almost," she says.

My back arches when she touches me. I feel her on top of me, around me, damp, soft, and hot. I groan with her when she holds and pushes my body against hers; I put my hands around her sweaty skin and hold and push her body, too.

When I feel her breathing quicken, I search for her tongue with mine.

"You're not trembling any more."

"No."

They were lying on the floor. She got up to put on Simone's shirt.

"A classic," she said. Simone stayed on the ground, flat on his back, his arms stretched out to the sides, as if on a cross.

"I can't look at you like that," she said and lay down next to him, placing one arm under his neck and wrapping her legs through his. Then she took one of his hands and placed it on her face.

"Don't you want to know what I look like?" she asked.

"No, it doesn't matter."

"They say I'm pretty. I have a small mole near my mouth that's supposed to be very sensual. Here. Touch it."

She took one of his fingers and ran it across her mouth, over the mole, then down to her lips again and kissed his fingertips.

"I don't usually like to touch people," Simone said.

"Not even me?"

"No, with you it's different. But listen, Grazia, don't talk to me about things that I can't understand. Body shape, eye color, hair. I don't understand things I can't see; they don't mean anything to me. I have my own colors and shapes. If I could only touch you, I would end up knowing only parts of you and I don't want that—even if I do like certain parts of you very much."

He ran his hand along Grazia's shoulder and down her back, across the curve of her hip and between her legs, where she was still warm. Grazia moaned.

"I like all of you. You're a smell. A sound. You're you."

"What do I smell like?"

"Oil, sweat, cotton, and 'Summertime.'"

"Doesn't sound too good," she said smiling.

"It's wonderful . . . I like it. But you want to know how I see you, so I'll tell you. I already know what you look like. Your skin is so clear I can put my fingers through it, and you have blue hair."

Grazia was silent. She slid her foot up and down

Simone's leg for a few seconds, then hugged him and kissed him quickly on the cheek.

"I don't know what that means, but it sounds nice. I'm going to jump in the shower."

Good evening, I'm Commissario Poletto. Could you tell me what room the blind man and the policewoman are in? Thank you. Excuse me, but is that an Exacto knife? Would you be so kind as to lend it to me?

Grazia slid the shower door open and leaned out as far as she could, listening. She kept her eyes shut because of the shampoo.

"Did you call me?"

She had left the bathroom and the bedroom doors open, but the sound of the water inside the shower stall was so loud that she could barely hear her own voice. She thought she had heard a sound—the telephone perhaps. She stepped out of the shower and walked on tiptoe to the bidet where she had left her gun, holding on to the sink so as not to slip. Blinking back the shampoo, she peered out the door.

Simone, still naked, was sitting on the armchair in the bedroom. From the way he moved his head she guessed he was listening to music, but she couldn't hear it because of the shower.

She wrapped her gun in one of the plastic bags the hotel provided, with "Please do not throw sanitary napkins into the WC" printed on it, and went back under the water, putting the gun on the shelf between the shampoo and the body soap. She looked up toward the nozzle and let the warm water spray her face, let it take her breath away. She filled her mouth with water and squirted the water against the shower door, the way she'd always done ever since she was a child.

She picked up the body soap and squeezed a little curl into the palm of her hand. She smiled as her hand and the pine-scented bubbles slid down her stomach and between her legs. She thought about Vittorio. What would he say? When would she tell him?

Something moved outside the door: a familiar, light-colored shadow, framed by the material of a raincoat with its collar raised. Instinctively, Grazia put one hand on the plastic bag where she had hid her gun, with the other hand she opened the shower door.

"Vittorio!" she said, with a sharp breath. Without warning the shadow hit her over the head, knocking her to the shower floor with one blow.

I got her.

I watch her fall to the floor, hands first. She tries to get up by holding onto the sides of the tub, but her legs slip back into the shower.

I kick her in the gut, making her groan. There's a bag on the floor, I bend down, pick it up, weigh it in my hand to see if it's heavy enough, then hit her on the head with it.

I get undressed calmly.

I go into the shower.

I let the water run down my shaved head and over

my headphones, I let it wash my hairless body all the
way down to where the Walkman hangs, crackling and
fizzling, between my legs.

The guitar and voices get distorted. They snake into
my ears, the tongue of a reptile, a downpour of electrifying rain, thunder that's getting closer, lightning that
splits the sky.

*"I won't take no prisoner, won't spare no lives . . . nobody's
putting up a fight . . . I got my bell, I'm gonna take you to
hell . . . I'm gonna get you, Satan'll get you . . ."*

Then "Hell's Bells" ends. The Walkman is silent—I
hear the bells of Satan inside my head.

I get out of the shower and look at my body.

The animal slithers under my skin, deforming my
face. My eyes sockets are empty: two dark cavities. My
lips peel back over my teeth in a dark howl.

The girl on the floor moves, she touches my ankle.

I turn around, pick up the heavy bag, and finish her
off.

That's not Grazia's footstep. Those aren't her naked
feet on the floor, not her skin pressing against the tiles.
Not her feet coming toward me on the carpet.

That's not Grazia.

There's someone in front of me. He's not saying
anything. He's just breathing. He smells strange. I'm
frightened.

Drops fall slowly to the carpet. I'm afraid.

The green voice.

"Hi. Remember me?"

He's looking at me but he doesn't see me.

He's looking through me. He's looking into me but he doesn't see anything.

I open my mouth, pull out my tongue, and show him the animal inside of me. It hisses at him, but he doesn't see it.

I get really close to him and lean my head against his. I want him to hear the bells but he can't.

I want to be like that.

I want to be like you.

I want to be you.

"Look—can you see it?" he says. I can tell that he has opened his mouth wide; the effort makes him gag and cough.

"Listen—can you hear it? Can you hear the bells?" he says, and leans his cold, wet face against mine, pulling my cheek and ear close to his.

I hear a small tapping sound, as if something is sliding over a ridgy surface.

"I want to be like that," he says.

"I want to be like you," he says.

"I want to be you," he says.

I smell metal.

I'm frightened.

Why is that cold naked woman jumping on me? Where did she come from? I thought I had killed her. She threw herself at my legs and knocked me down. She's climbing on my back, howling like an animal, choking me. She's got her legs wrapped around me, she's pinning me down with all her weight, grabbing at my neck with both hands. I'm suffocating. I can't breathe. Her thumbs push at my throat, her fingers squeeze my neck, my throat is closing, I can't breathe. I grab her wrists, scratch at her back and shoulders and try to push her away. Her face is covered with blood. I pull her hair but she doesn't let up, she's got my legs blocked, she's got a hold on my ankles with her feet. She's pushing her forehead down on mine and choking me—I can't breathe.

I open my mouth; my tongue slides out. If I could show her the animal maybe she'd let go, but her fingernails are planted in me like hooks, her fingers are crushing my throat, the animal can't get out. I want to hit her. I want to smash my beak into her face and kill her, but she's got me pinned down with her sweaty forehead. I feel her breath on me. She's breathing hard. I try and breathe but I can't—I'm choking, I can't breathe.

Grazia kept a hold on his throat even though she was seeing double. She could barely keep her head up. A red veil of blood blocked her vision. She breathed heavily but kept squeezing. She kept squeezing even when one of his hands scratched her back. Then it flopped off to the side. His other hand dug into her face and hair. She knew she was about to faint. She concentrated on the choking sound, trying to break it with her force. She squeezed his neck until her strength failed her. Her fingers let up, the red veil filled her head and Grazia passed out, her hands around his neck. Her head rolled off the Iguana's forehead, over his inert arms, and slowly, almost gently, to the floor.

I heard a wet smack and muffled punches. Figures moving in front of me. I heard the rough tumble of bodies on the carpeted floor. Bodies fighting. The smell of bodies fighting. I heard Grazia clench her teeth and groan. I heard her breathing the way she did when we made love. Then I heard a long, slow, throaty rattle. Then nothing. Silence. Total silence. I bend down on one knee and feel the carpet.

"Grazia? Grazia, where are you?"

And then that deep, raucous rattle. It's coming from someone's throat. From some thing's throat. The snarl of an animal. An animal that's still alive.

I push her off me and shake my hand to get rid of her hair. She almost killed me, but then she passed out. I could kill her now but it doesn't matter anymore. I'll be quick.

The blind man is on the floor, groping and clawing at the air. He freezes when he hears me stand up in front of him.

I pick up the Exacto knife that I dropped when the girl jumped on me and walk over to him and stand behind him.

I grab his hair and pull his head back. His whole body stiffens. I place my knee in the middle of his back to keep him still.

The bells are ringing louder than ever before. They explode inside my head and hammer at my eardrums. They are forcing my eyes out of their sockets. The death bells make my head roll.

The animal is crazed now. It pulls up the skin of my face. My lips and forehead are swollen, my jaw is out of place. I can barely speak.

I want to be like that, I say, smoothing his hair off his face.

I want to be like you, I say, grabbing him under the chin so he can't move.

I want to be you, I say.

Then I bring the blade to my eyes and jab it in.

God, that scream! I will never forget that scream. It wasn't human—it was so green it scratched the ceiling, filled the room, and reverberated off the walls. It went on and on. I felt his fingers clutching at my chin. I felt warm, hard drops of liquid dripping onto my face. A howl came tearing out of his throat, it scraped across his teeth, it went on and on—

That scream!

Underfoot, I feel the stubble of freshly cut grass.
Green.
Above, I smell the fresh, cool summer sky.
Blue.
I hold a big, round, smooth apple in my hand.
Red.
I grope through the air until I feel the cold metal backrest of the park bench. I slide my hand along its cracked surface, gauging the length of the seat with my leg. I follow it until I reach the distant corner, then choose where to sit. I sit down slowly, first with the palm of my hand, then the rest of me. But when I touch the seat with my hand, the apple slips out of my grasp. I freeze and listen to where it will fall even before it touches the ground.

It's on the grass, to the left. I hear it roll back toward me. I bend down and pick it up on my first try. Then I walk away—voices are coming toward me.

I don't want to talk, or listen, to anyone. Especially to that policewoman who asked to see me.

I want to be alone.

Later I'll go back to my room and listen to a little music.

Jazz.

Be-bop.

Chet Baker.

They gave me a CD but I would have preferred a record. On a record you can feel the grooves with your finger and choose the song, but you can't feel anything on a CD. Besides, the CD player is hard to use. The buttons aren't in relief. There are too many options. I asked someone to cut out some shapes for me to stick on the buttons but they keep falling off.

There's one song that I really like but I have to listen to all the other songs first.

"Almost Blue."

Blue.

Sometimes when I listen to it, I fall asleep on the chair in front of my window. If it's sunny outside, it feels like a thousand miniature fishhooks are pulling at my skin. They say I have fair skin. They say I burn easily.

Sometimes, when I go to bed at night, the dark seems even darker than usual. That only happens when the lightbulb in the emergency exit sign is out. They say I can still see slight variations in light. But it doesn't happen often, though, because here at the prison hospital you're not allowed to turn off the emergency exit light — ever.

Sometimes a shiver runs through me, under my skin. The doctor says it's just a little bit of fever, a side effect from the 50mm dose of Serenase I take every two weeks.

As for the bells, well, I don't hear them anymore.

The sound of a record dropping onto a turntable is like a short sigh, with a touch of dust mixed in. The sound of the automated arm rising up from its rest is like a repressed hiccup or a tongue clucking drily—a plastic tongue. The needle, as it glides across the grooves, sibilates softly, then crackles once or twice. Then comes the piano, the bass, and finally the velvety voice of Chet Baker singing "Almost Blue."

Simone could hear her coming as soon as she was at the bottom of the stairs, even when she tried to be as quiet as possible. She had been out of the hospital for only two days and still needed to hold onto the banister to keep her balance. The banister creaks.

As soon as he heard her, he'd turn off the scanners. He'd turn down Chet Baker. He'd uncross his legs, swivel around in his chair, and raise his face toward the door, as if he could see her come in. His face always pointed a little to the left.

He'd smile if it suddenly got quiet. He knew she was trying to trick him by stopping to take off her boots. But her shoelaces gave her away. The way the step creaked when she sat down to take off her boots gave her away. The crick in her knee gave her away.

He was always ready to hear the door handle turn.

Then Grazia would be in the attic. And with her came that perfume: oil, sweat, cotton, and "Summertime." The music accompanied her everywhere; he would begin hearing it as soon as she started climbing the stairs.

Even though he couldn't see her, Simone knew exactly what Grazia looked like.

Her skin was so clear he could poke his fingers through it, and she had blue hair.